THE STANDOFF

"Now you're a big cowman, Jake," I said. "You're hiring cheap killers. That's what it takes to be a big cowman, isn't it?"

"You ought to know," Murdock said.

"That's right," I said. "I've been one, and I've seen plenty of them. I can spot them a mile off. Now get that son-of-a-bitch off my back or I'll blow his brains out."

Bunker snickered. "Try it, friend. Try it."

His right hand hovered over the butt of his gun. He'd be fast, I thought, but not fast enough. You never face a man like that thinking he might be fast enough, or sooner or later you'll run into one who was.

I started to turn toward Bunker. That was all it took. He went for his gun....

BITTER WIND

WAYNE D. OVERHOLSER

LEISURE BOOKS  NEW YORK CITY

A LEISURE BOOK®

October 2007

Published by special arrangement with Golden West Literary Agency.

Dorchester Publishing Co., Inc.
200 Madison Avenue
New York, NY 10016

ISBN 10: 0-8439-5841-3
ISBN 13: 978-0-8439-5841-6

The name "Leisure Books" and the stylized "L" with design are trademarks of Dorchester Publishing Co., Inc.

Printed in the United States of America.

Visit us on the web at www.dorchesterpub.com.

BITTER WIND

Chapter One

Jake Murdock saved my life before I ever saw him. I'm not sure about why he did the things he did. All I am sure about is that our lives were so intertwined from the day we met until his death that it is hard to tell which one of us had the most influence on the other.

It started on a cold, windy day in late March, 1876. I was just twenty-one, but already the name Bill Lang meant something. I had made enough of a reputation as a gunfighter to hold a job with a big cattle outfit in southern Colorado just out of Trinidad. We had a range war going and I'd been earning fighting wages until a county election brought in a new sheriff. After that I found it expedient to leave the country.

Most of the men who had been working with me dropped south into New Mexico, but I'd had some trouble down there and I decided to ride the other way into Wyoming. I'd spent a year on Powder River with an old mountain man named Burke

Teller, so I knew a little bit about the country and I liked it.

Besides, there is always a question of where a man is going when he has to move. I didn't care much for Kansas or Nebraska and I figured the Mormons wouldn't welcome me if I landed up in Utah. The Texas Rangers were anxious to have my company, but I didn't want theirs, so Wyoming seemed the logical place. The only thing was I had forgotten how far it was from Trinidad to Cheyenne, especially in March with six inches of snow on the ground.

Cheyenne looked good to me. Real good. I hadn't hurried out of Colorado, but there were a couple of dead men down there on the Picketwire, and sooner or later that long-nosed sheriff in Trinidad was going to put one and one together and figure out it made two, me and another gunslinger who was in Santa Fé by this time. No, I sure hadn't hurried, but I hadn't let any grass grow under the hoofs of my buckskin gelding, either.

I left my horse in a livery stable with orders to give him a double bait of oats, thinking I wouldn't be forking him for a week at least. I took a room in the Inter-Ocean Hotel on Sixteenth Street and sat down at a table in the dining room and had a steak a foot long, four cups of coffee, and a slab of apple pie.

After that I felt like a new man. I stepped into a saloon, had one drink, and took a hand in a poker game. My luck ran high. I raked in three pots in a row that added up to better than one hundred dollars, and I asked myself why I risked my hide in a range war when I could get rich in a poker game. Then it happened.

The man sitting across from me was tall and skinny with two very black eyes crowding a saber-sharp nose. His skin was dark. I've seen Indians who weren't much darker, so I figured he was a half-breed. He was young, about my age, I judged. I didn't know who he was and I didn't care.

The saloon was crowded with soldiers from Fort D.A. Russell, cowboys, freighters, townsmen, and Black Hillers waiting for the weather to break so they could hit the road north. One minute there was a lot of racket going on—loud talk and glasses clinking and a piano player knocking out "Yellow Rose of Texas"—then all of a sudden the racket stopped and I didn't hear a sound except the heavy breathing of many men.

The skinny fellow had shoved his chair back and he'd said, loud and clear: "I seen how you dealt that last hand. You're a cheating son-of-a-bitch."

The other men at the table spilled out of their chairs so fast you'd have thought a swarm of bees had moved in on them. I guess everybody in the room got the word judging by the way the noise stopped. I still didn't know who the skinny man was and I still didn't care because, when you've lived the kind of life I had for the last three years, you get so you figure you can handle any tough hand who comes along.

This fellow was a tough hand, all right. He sat there staring at me, his black eyes boring into mine while he waited for me to make a move. A couple of men standing at the bar started toward me, then changed their minds and stopped and backed up to the bar. After that they just stood there, watching.

Hell, I wasn't looking for trouble. All I'd wanted

was to get out of the wind and have a drink and a few hands of poker. I hadn't cheated. As a matter of fact, I never had cheated at cards. It just didn't seem worthwhile. If I was going to cheat, I'd cheat big the way cattlemen and politicians do. But it was not a proposition of me looking for trouble. Here it was, in full bloom right in front of me.

I didn't have any choice. I got up out of my chair and pulled my gun and I drilled the skinny man right between the eyes. He was out of his chair, too, and he yanked his gun out of leather, but when he pulled the trigger, he was dead and going down. All his bullet did was to bore a hole in the green top of the poker table.

As soon as I holstered my gun, I looked around to see if there was a lawman in the place because I wanted to be cleared then and there. It took a few seconds for the crowd to catch up with what had happened. The men acted as if they were stunned, then a dozen or more came up and shook hands and patted me on the back and told me to get the hell out of Cheyenne.

When I could make myself heard, I asked: "Why should I get out of Cheyenne? Do you arrest a man for shooting in self-defense?"

One of the men who had been standing at the bar and had started toward me was a businessman. He looked important, a banker maybe. He wore a brown broadcloth suit and an elk's tooth that dangled from a gold chain that hung across his vest.

"No, we don't," this fellow said. "If you were arrested, you would soon be released on the grounds of justifiable homicide. The proposition is that the man you just killed is one of the Flynn brothers. Old

Mike Flynn has a ranch on Pole Creek. He'll never forgive you for killing his boy. One of his cowhands took out of here just now, so Mike will hear about it in two, three hours. He'll saddle up along with the rest of his sons and they'll come after you."

I didn't like the notion of running and I said so. Another man, a judge, I figured, was tall and appeared very impressive with his white hair and white beard and mustache. He said with a hint of a Southern drawl: "Mister, you're a stranger in town. Chances are you don't know anything about the Flynns. Old Mike's got a Sioux squaw who's the mother of his six boys. They're tough. They're more like their mother's people than they are old Mike's. You can't hope to fight all of them and live to tell about it."

I still didn't get the full picture. I said: "I've bucked long odds before and I'm still alive. I've been riding four, five days and I'm tired."

They looked at each other and swallowed and shifted around from one foot to the other, then the man I took for a judge cleared his throat. He said: "Mister, you're going to have to ride a little more. If you're still in Cheyenne, the Flynn outfit will come to town and tear it apart. We don't want that to happen again. We don't owe you anything, so, to save your life and us a lot of trouble, get on your horse and slope out of here."

The man with the elk's tooth on his watch chain nodded. "Why don't you take a sashay up to Fort Laramie? The Flynns never go there. They don't get along with the Army very well. In fact, they don't get along with the ranchers up there on the Chug very well, either."

I didn't care much about fighting the town of Cheyenne and it began to look as if it was going to stack up that way. It didn't take any smart man to see that this bunch wasn't as friendly as it had been a few minutes before. They sure didn't want the Flynn outfit coming into town to find me. For them it was a simple proposition of taking on one man instead of Flynn and his sons.

"That's a good idea," I said to the man with the elk's tooth. "I'll probably like Fort Laramie."

I left the saloon, got my war sack out of the hotel room I'd rented, paid at the desk for a bed I hadn't used, and saddled my buckskin and rode north. I thought I'd make it to Fort Laramie in two days, but I was wrong. It was two months before I saw the place.

Chapter Two

I don't know of any other part of the country where the wind blows the way it does around Cheyenne. I was wearing my sheepskin and gloves, and I had my head pulled down into my coat collar turtle-like, but, in spite of everything I could do, I was still cold. The wind seemed to cut right down into the marrow of my bones.

Some of the ground had been blown bare of snow, but in other places the snow had piled up in deep drifts. If they were in the road as some of them were, I had to ride around them. Most of the time the wind picked up so much snow that the air was filled with it and I couldn't see more than fifty feet in any direction. I figured the snow wasn't coming down to the ground until it reached Nebraska.

About the middle of the afternoon the wind died and I could see the horizon in all directions. I had crossed Pole Creek, so the Flynn Ranch had to be south of me. I hadn't thought about it and I hadn't thought much about being followed, but now I saw that a horseman was behind me.

I pulled off into a nest of willows and waited, but he didn't show up. I thought that, if I had seen him in the saloon, I'd jump him as soon as he rode up and ask him what he was doing on a day like this that wasn't fit for man or beast, but I guess he knew I was waiting for him. After I went on, I looked back and there he was just about the same distance behind me that he had been all the time.

Near dark I came to a road ranch and pulled into the yard and asked if I could get a meal and a bed. I guess not much traffic to the Black Hills had come out of Cheyenne because these people were glad to see me and said of course I could have a meal and a bed. A boy stepped out of the barn and took my buckskin, saying he'd rub him down and see he had a good feeding.

When I went into the house, my hands were so cold I had trouble unbuttoning my sheepskin. I finally got it off and hung it and my hat on a peg near the door, then I stood in front of the fireplace and rubbed my hands together until the circulation came back. If the fellow following me was looking for a fight, I would have the advantage of getting thawed out first.

I was hoping he wouldn't stop. I just didn't want any more trouble. Sometimes I had a feeling that I was a magnet that attracted trouble because it came too often to me just the way it had back there in Cheyenne. If I had taken a hand in some other poker game, nothing would have happened. No one but young Flynn would have accused me of cheating, and I'd have stayed in town until the weather warmed up just as I planned. But it hadn't worked that way.

I've thought about this a lot and I've never come to any solid conclusion, but it does seem that a man's life takes on a certain pattern, and the longer he follows that pattern, the harder it is to change it. Not that I wanted to change mine. I saw nothing wrong with the way I'd been living, but there wasn't any point in risking my hide when I wasn't getting paid for it.

This time nature brought about a little change in the pattern. When the man came in, he didn't have any fight in him. It had been frozen right out of his guts if he'd had any in the first place. He had trouble getting out of his coat, and, after he finally succeeded in pulling it off, he stumbled to the fireplace and stood beside me with his hands out, his teeth chattering.

He was a runt of a man with watery eyes and not much nose and a weak chin. He carried a gun, but I had a hunch he wouldn't have used it under any circumstances. Chances are he didn't know how. The more I studied him, the surer I was he didn't have any interest in me. The way he acted, you'd have thought I wasn't standing there beside him.

The fellow kept on shivering as if he were coming down with chills and fever. Even after the rancher called us into the dining room for supper, the runt kept on shivering. It wasn't until he had two cups of steaming coffee in him that he appeared to thaw out.

No one talked much. The woman was a good cook. She had antelope steak, biscuits, honey, beans, lots of hot coffee, and prune pie for dessert. Cooking was a big chore for her because she had six kids to feed besides me and the runt. With her and her husband, there were ten of us at the table.

When we finished eating, I sat there, rolled and smoked a cigarette, just feeling warm and relaxed and comfortable, but the runt went back into the other room. I supposed he wanted to hug the fireplace again, but when I drifted into the room, he was gone. His hat and coat were gone, too.

The rancher was reading a newspaper.

I asked: "Where did our sawed-off friend go?"

The rancher looked at me as if the question made him uneasy, then he said: "He ain't staying the night. He just wanted his supper, then he pulled out."

When I heard that, I wasn't so sure about his following me. To go back into that wind was crazy, especially for a man who'd been as cold as he was. The wind had died down some, so it wouldn't be as cold as it had been, but still the runt must have had some mighty urgent business to keep riding.

I rolled another cigarette, turning this over in my mind and not liking what I turned up. Finally I asked: "Where's the Flynn spread?"

The rancher put his newspaper down. He scratched a cheek, taking his time to answer. There wasn't any doubt about him being uneasy now. He said: "Funny you'd ask that. That there other fellow asked the same question. Told me he got acquainted with one of the Flynn boys in Cheyenne and had been told he could get a job there, but he guessed he'd ridden past the turn-off with the ground blizzard blowing the way it was."

"It was pretty bad today," I said. "Where did you say the Flynn Ranch was?"

"Over yonder." He pointed southwest. "Ain't far. Six, eight miles from here. He won't have no trouble finding it if the wind stays down." He shook his head, his expression going sour. "They're a bad bunch, them Flynns. I don't know why anybody would want to work for 'em. They ain't bothered me, but they've robbed some of the ranchers blind up north of here."

I knew, then. The runt had been following me. He'd been given orders in Cheyenne to trail me. Now for a price he was trying to get to the Flynn Ranch to tell the old man where I was. I'd said back there in the saloon that I'd bucked long odds and I was still alive. It was true, but I wasn't anxious to do it again. If the runt found the Flynn place in time, I'd have them on my tail before I left.

"What time do you have breakfast?" I asked.

"Six o'clock," the rancher answered.

"I'll pull out right after I eat," I said.

He nodded, relieved. "I'll call you. I'll show you your room and you can go to bed or come back down and keep the fire warm if you want to."

"I'll go to bed," I said.

I was out of there in the morning right after breakfast with no sign of the Flynns. The wind was gone, the sky was deep blue, and, when I rode up to the top of one of those long swells in the prairie, I could see to hell and gone. Sooner or later the Flynns would show up. I didn't doubt it, but I still didn't know for sure what I'd do.

I kept watching behind me, and along toward noon I spotted them. Not much snow here, and the ground was dry enough for them to raise a little dust. At first the dust was all I could see, then they gained on me and I could make them out. I counted six riders.

I knew I couldn't outrun them to Fort Laramie. Their horses were fresh and fast, and mine was tired. I turned this over in my mind for a while, and I didn't like what turned up this time, either. If I didn't find a place to hole up, I'd be a dead man. With six of them after me, maybe I was anyway.

About an hour later I crossed Chugwater Creek and I could see a white cliff off to my left, maybe fifty feet high with a nest of boulders at the bottom. The Flynn bunch had almost closed the gap and now they began shooting at me. They were too far away to be accurate, but it's never a comfortable feeling to be shot at. You don't know when a lucky shot can raise hell. That's exactly what happened.

I must have been fifty yards from the boulders when one of their bullets caught my horse right through the head. He went down in a plunging, kicking fall. I got clear, but I was shaken up some and it took me a little while to get my Winchester out of the boot. I started for the boulders on the dead run, and that came close to being a fatal mistake.

The Flynn horses were a little winded, but they could still move faster than I could run. I thought I was going to make it. I almost did. I wasn't more than six or eight feet from the nearest boulder when a bullet smashed through the meaty part of my right thigh and I went down.

The slugs were kicking up dust all around me. I crawled and dived to the nearest boulder and rolled behind it. I had moved as fast as I could, but with that smashed-up leg, it wasn't very fast.

Somehow I got to my feet, or foot, because I had to put all my weight on my left leg. The Flynns were whipping their horses and coming in six abreast, riding as fast as they could make their horses go. They must have thought I was about done for and wanted to finish me off in a hurry and get out of there. I raised my rifle, figuring I'd get one or two before they reached my boulder, but I didn't pull the trigger.

Somebody on top of the cliff above me started shooting. I swear I never saw anything like it. Whoever it was fired four times as fast as he could squeeze the trigger and lever another shell into the chamber. Every shot took a Flynn out of his saddle. Four of them, just as if some invisible force had gone right down the line and tumbled each one off his horse.

Three of them hit the ground and didn't move. The fourth one got to his feet and staggered a couple of steps, then he went down and didn't move again. The two on my left, one a white man with a beard and the other a dark-skinned boy younger than the one I'd shot in Cheyenne, wheeled their horses and took out of there on the run.

I'd figured I was a goner. Now I had a reprieve, but I had a hunch I was going to bleed to death right there. I could feel the warm flow of blood running down my leg. I set my Winchester down and took out my knife and slit my pants leg. The bullet hadn't smashed the bone and had gone on through, but it had played hell with the flesh of that thigh. The blood wasn't spurting, so the bullet hadn't severed an artery, but I was losing blood pretty fast just the same.

I wadded up my bandanna and slapped it over the bullet hole as a man rode down the slope. He'd had to circle a little to get down off the top of the cliff. Now he reined up in front of me. My eyes didn't focus right, so I didn't have much notion what he looked like except that he was big and rode a roan horse and had a sweeping reddish-brown mustache.

He took one look at my leg and stepped down. "Here," he said, "I'll help you up. My house is yonder a little ways." He pointed to it. "The horse will take you there. My squaw Ellie will get the blood stopped. I'll fetch your saddle."

I wasn't very clear about a lot of things after that. Somehow he got me into the saddle and I vaguely remember jolting along and trying to hold that wadded-up bandanna over the bullet hole. Then the horse stopped and a door opened and a screen slammed. I saw a woman standing in front of the house. She didn't look like any squaw I'd ever seen. She was white, so I figured I'd heard wrong, but then I was sure I hadn't.

I said something about bleeding to death, or thought I said it, and that was all. I slid out of the saddle and I remember falling and falling, but I don't remember hitting the ground.

Chapter Three

When I came to, it was dark. For a while everything was blurred in my mind and I couldn't remember what had happened or where I was. Then it came back. The big man on top of the cliff and how he'd knocked over four of the Flynns and his putting me on his horse and the horse bringing me to a house. That must be where I was.

The furniture in the room came clear finally. I was lying on a bunk in a corner. A rawhide-bottom chair was beside me, and my clothes, saddle, Winchester, and gun belt were piled neatly in the corner. A range and table were in the other end of the room.

On beyond the stove was a small work table and a number of shelves filled with cans and sacks of food. A young woman stood at the range, frying meat. Then I remembered the big man's talking about his squaw Ellie and the woman who had come through the door just as I rode up.

For a long time I lay there and looked at the woman. It seemed like a long time anyhow. I could see enough of her to know she wasn't a squaw. When I began to move around a little, she heard me and whirled and came quickly to the side of the bunk.

"You be quiet," she said sternly. "I had a hard time getting the blood stopped, but I finally found enough cobwebs to do it. Now you lie still or you'll start the bleeding again."

I was weak and my thigh hurt, but I wasn't so bad off I couldn't appreciate a pretty woman. She was my age or maybe younger, with dark brown hair and dark eyes, and skin that was light brown, about the color a white woman's would be if she were out in sun every day.

Her features were just about perfect, I thought. There was a sweetness about her mouth that I had seldom seen on the face of any woman, and never on a half-breed. They were a discontented lot most of the time. Of course, she might not be a half-breed, but the big man had called her his squaw, so she must be a half-breed. I was dead sure she wasn't a full-blooded Indian.

"Are you Ellie?" I asked.

"I'm Ellie," she answered. "Now I've got to finish those antelope steaks because Jake will be in pretty soon and he'll be hungry and mad if supper isn't ready. He'll be madder if they're burned." She went back to the stove and said over her shoulder: "I've fixed some chicken broth for you. I'll come and feed you as soon as these steaks are done."

"I can feed myself," I said, sharp-like.

I had a tight bandage on my right thigh and all my clothes were off except my drawers. She must have undressed me, I thought, and then I wondered if she had got me into bed by herself.

She glanced at me and laughed. When a man isn't real sure of himself, he has to speak up big and proud to prove he's still a man. I'm not sure he proves it to anyone else, but he proves it to himself and that's important. I guess that's the way it was with me and she seemed to understand that.

"All right," she said. "Feed yourself. I've got plenty to do."

She poured the broth into a bowl and brought it to me. She set it on the floor and picked up a couple of pillows that were in a rocking chair by the window.

"If you can lift your head a little," she said, "I'll slip these pillows under it. It'll make it easier for you to eat."

I didn't have any idea how weak I was, just lying there on my back the way I had been, but I must have lost a lot more blood than I'd thought. By the time I had those pillows under my head and she'd handed me the bowl of broth and a spoon, I was ready to have her feed me, but I was damned if I was going to say so. She went back to the stove and I fed myself, although there were times when I wasn't real sure I was strong enough to lift the spoonful of broth from the bowl to my mouth.

I had finished and was lying there, too tired to pull the pillows out from under my head, when the big man came in. He clapped his hands together and said: "Hot damn, it's colder'n a witch's tit to-night." He pulled off his gloves and looked at me and saw I was awake. He came to the bunk and held out his hand. "I'm Jake Murdock. I'm glad to see you alive and kicking."

I shook hands. I mean, I held mine up and he just about squeezed it off at the wrist. I said: "I'm Bill

Lang." As far as he was concerned, it might as well have been John Smith. He'd never heard of me.

He peeled off his coat and hung it and his hat on the antler rack near the door; then he came over to the bunk and stood looking down at me while he chewed on his lower lip. He said: "What fetched that Flynn wolf pack after you? They ain't in the habit of coming so far north in the daytime."

I told him, making the story as short as I could because I didn't have the steam to make it any longer. When I finished, he asked: "Which Flynn was it you plugged?"

"I dunno."

"What'd he look like?"

"Skinny," I answered. "No lips much. Sharpnosed. Pretty young, maybe twenty or twenty-one."

He kept looking down at me, a hint of admiration in his gray eyes. He was a big man, in his late twenties or maybe even thirty. Every time he took a breath, his barrel of a chest heaved up until it strained the buttons on his shirt and the cloth in front got as tight as the top of a drum. His arms were as big as my thighs. His hair was reddish brown about the same as his mustache.

I handed my empty bowl to him as I said: "Would you pull the pillows out from under my head?"

"Sure." He took the bowl and I lifted my head an inch or so, and he jerked the pillows off the bunk. "Lang, you're new to this country, ain't you?"

"I'd been in Cheyenne an hour or so," I said. "The last thing I was looking for was trouble."

He laughed, a short, jerky laugh. "When you're around any of the Flynns, you don't have to look for trouble. It looks for you."

He tossed the pillows onto the rocking chair and took the empty bowl to the work table near the far wall.

Ellie said: "Jake, your supper's ready."

Murdock acted as if he hadn't heard. He came back to my bunk. "The one you shot was called Darb. What you don't know is that he was the gunman of the family. If he hadn't been dead sure he'd outdraw you, he'd never have called for a showdown. He's killed several men in gunfights, three that I know of for sure. If he was looking for a fight and you outdrew him, you're a fast man with a gun. That's all I've got to say."

"Jake, your supper's ready," Ellie said again.

Murdock grunted something and turned around and walked to the table. He looked as if he didn't fully believe what I'd told him. He didn't say a word until he and Ellie finished eating, and then he got up and came to my bunk and sat down on the rawhide-bottom chair.

"I'm sorry about your horse," he said. "I might have saved him if I'd opened up sooner, but I probably wouldn't have hit any of 'em at that distance. To tell the truth, I didn't want to start shooting until I was sure I could whittle the odds down. The last thing I wanted to do was to tangle with six Flynns."

"It was lucky for me you were up on that cliff," I said. "I wasn't in any shape to fight them off."

"You weren't for a fact," he agreed. "I've been looking for a chance to shoot a few Flynns. We've figured for quite a while that most of the raids and killings we've been laying onto the Sioux was really the Flynns. Proving it was something else, but one thing's sure now. They won't bother us no more."

He took his pipe out of his pocket, filled it, and tamped the tobacco down. When he had it going, I asked: "I don't want to run you out of your bed. If you've got a shed or a barn where I could . . ."

"You stay right there," he said. "We've got two rooms. When Ellie first came, I just had this one, so I built another room on for sleeping, and we cook and eat in here."

There was no door leading from this room into the other one, so they had to step outside to go from one to the other. I'd seen houses like this before. They were really two cabins built together, and I could never understand a man's reasoning when he added on in this manner, but I had no intention of asking Murdock about it.

Maybe he read my mind because after he puffed a while, he said: "This is just our temporary house, though we've been in it four years, so it ain't real temporary. Later on we'll use it for a bunkhouse and we'll build a big, two-story place a little closer to the Chug."

He puffed some more, and then he said: "I've got to put my hands on a little money. Well, more'n a little money. I want to buy a herd of cattle. I'm sitting right here in the best damned cattle country in the world and I ain't in position to take advantage of it."

I understood that. The cattle business was just starting in Wyoming and Montana and it was bound to grow as men with money moved into the country. I knew a little bit about the Indian problem up here. As soon as the Sioux and Cheyennes were whipped, and that wouldn't be long the way the Black Hills situation was stacking up, the empty range would be taken.

He rose. "Ellie's got the dishes done," he said, "so we'll go to bed. I guess you won't be going anywhere tonight."

"I sure won't," I said.

He took his pipe out of his mouth and looked down at me for several seconds. Finally he said: "I hope you'll stay here for a spell. Don't get any ideas you've got to move on just to be riding. Ellie won't mind looking after you."

"Thanks," I said. "I'll have to stay a while anyway."

He put his pipe into his mouth and left the room. Ellie blew out the lamp and followed him. I lay on my back and stared into the darkness, my thigh hurting like the devil. I don't think I slept much all night. I had a lot of things on my mind and that was good because it kept me from thinking about the pain in my leg. Mostly I kept wondering about Ellie and how Murdock had ever got hold of a girl as pretty as she was.

Chapter Four

I didn't get out of that bunk for several days. To a man who had looked after himself as long as I had and who hadn't been around any woman who could be called a "good" woman for a while, it was just plain humiliating to have Ellie look after me the way she did, but she didn't seem to mind.

She attended to her business of cooking and washing and cleaning house and nursing me with a smile and all the time looking as pretty as a filly hitched up to a brand new red-wheeled buggy. Most of the time she was humming, sweet haunting tunes I had never heard before in my life.

Murdock didn't seem to worry about leaving her with me. I guessed he realized I wasn't in any shape to be interested in her, and, after I got better, I think he knew we were going to be friends. I'm not sure he knew it, but I did right from the first.

After a few days I was able to spend most of my waking hours in a chair. Murdock fixed me up with a crutch so I could hobble across the room or to the table, and after that Ellie didn't have to wait on me hand and foot the way she had been.

Murdock worked hard, although at the time I didn't know what he was doing. He was gone all morning and all afternoon, and sometimes all day, but most of the time he'd be home for dinner. I could tell it had been a pretty lonely life for Ellie, with the nearest neighbor three miles away, but she never complained. We didn't talk much the first few days because I hurt so damned much I didn't feel like talking, and Ellie must have sensed that. She didn't run off at the mouth the way some women do, a characteristic I liked.

One time I heard a man say that the only tool in the world that gets sharper with constant use is a woman's tongue, and it sure is the truth. I guess it's one reason some men don't stay home any more than they have to, but Ellie had a way of knowing when I wanted to talk and it was the same with Murdock when he was there.

It didn't take me long to figure out some things. One was the simple fact that Murdock took Ellie for granted the way some men take an old shoe for granted. Jake Murdock was an honest, hard-working man. He was moral by his own standards, and I guess this varies with different men.

I could see right from the first that Ellie was in love with Murdock, but like I said, he took her for granted. It seemed to me it wasn't right. A situation like that was bound to raise hell sooner or later, and it did.

One afternoon I was sitting by the window, looking out toward the Chugwater, when Ellie brought a pair of Murdock's pants she'd been mending and pulled her chair up beside mine. I was feeling real pert now and the truth was she bothered me. I hadn't touched her except by accident a time or two, but I didn't have to touch her to know she had a soft, attractive body.

I guess I got a little red in the face and I turned my head and looked out across the pasture that still had a few spots of snow. We were in the last week of March, and the calendar claimed it was spring, but it must not have been a Wyoming calendar.

When I finally looked at Ellie, she was sewing away and smiling as if she were the happiest woman in the territory. One thing was sure. She wasn't bothered one bit sitting there about a foot from me. I suspected then, and later found out I was right, that Ellie accepted sex as something a man needed, on about the same level as eating and sleeping.

It wasn't a question of morals with her; there wasn't any right or wrong about it. I don't think she even gave it a thought. But she wasn't the kind who would get into bed with any man. Just the ones she liked, and there were only the two of us she liked that well.

I sat there, getting goose pimples all over me. I had a notion that all I needed to do was to ask Ellie to get into the bunk with me and she'd do it, but I wasn't going to. Jake Murdock had saved my life and taken me into his home and he was a hell of a fine man. What kind of a sneaky, double-crosser would that have made me?

All of a sudden Ellie said: "One of these days Jake is going to marry me. He promised he would."

It was the first words she'd said since she'd moved over there beside me. I just about fell out of

my chair. I turned and looked at her. Naturally I had
assumed they were married, although I had noticed
she wasn't wearing a wedding ring.

"I'd supposed you were married," I said.

She shook her head. "No. Most ranchers here-
abouts don't marry their squaws. They're what's
called men of the country."

I'd never heard the expression, but then I'd never
lived in this part of Wyoming before. I said: "You're
no squaw."

She looked up from her sewing. "Oh, yes, I am,"
she said. "My skin's white enough so I could pass
for a white woman. I did when I was a girl, but I'm a
quarter-breed Sioux and I'm not ashamed of it. In
fact, I'd be ashamed to pretend I was anything else.
I've got a brother named Charley Three Horses who
works for a neighbor. He's a lot darker than I am,
but everybody on the Chug knows he's my brother."

"Jake ought to marry you," I said angrily. "What's
he waiting for?"

She smiled. "Oh, I dunno. He just never got
around to it. Jake's got a one-track mind. He's always figuring on how he's going to make a big
spread out of the JM, but he needs big money and he
doesn't know where to get it. That's the only thing
that's important to him. I mention getting married
once in a while and he'll say we'll go to Cheyenne
next week or next month and do it, but when the
time comes, he's got other things to do."

"You ought to leave him," I said.

She looked up, alarm in her face. "Oh, no. I'll take
what I can get and be happy. A lot of the ranchers
around here are sending their squaws back to the
reservation and then the white men go to Cheyenne

and hunt for a white wife. When they first took their squaws, there weren't any white women in the country, but there are now. It's hard to find a good white wife, though. Some of the ranchers go to the whorehouses and what have they got when they get married? A lazy wife. That's what."

It struck me that she didn't think being a whore was immoral, but being a lazy wife was. I filled my pipe and fired it, and thought about that notion for a while. Maybe she was right as far as this ranch country was concerned.

I guess you can always get an argument over whether or not whoring is a moral profession, but nobody can argue that a lazy wife is moral. Maybe it's the same proposition as considering an ordinary killing of a man a misdemeanor, but horse stealing is a felony and they hang a man for doing it.

After a while my thoughts got back to Ellie and I asked: "Did you ever live on the reservation?"

She nodded. "Not since I was a little girl, though. My grandfather was an Irishman named Kelly. He killed a man in Saint Louis and got away and came up the river. He lived with my grandmother for about a year and then somebody heard where he was and they came and got him and took him back to Saint Louis and hung him. Seems like he'd killed an important fur trader. It was the wrong man. If it had been a nobody, they wouldn't have bothered with him."

It was an old story, I thought. You kill an important man and they'll have your hide every time. There ought to be a lesson somewhere in it for me, but then I'd killed a man on the Picketwire who wasn't important. Just a poor bastard of a homesteader who was living on a piece of land the cattle company wanted.

My trouble was the new sheriff who wanted to make a name for himself, and arresting a gunslinger named Bill Lang would do it, so I had to run or tangle with the sheriff and there was no percentage for me in that. A man couldn't win, I thought, not unless he had money and a hell of a lot of it. Money bought power, and, if you had enough power, you could do anything.

I asked: "Who was your father?"

"A Swede named Ole Johnson," she answered. "My mother died when I was ten. I remember her real well. She had light skin. Not as light as mine, but lighter than anyone else in our village. My father had lived with the Sioux for several years. I guess he just liked our ways because I never heard he was running from the law. Anyhow, he fell in love with my mother and they lived together until I was five. He got killed in a fight with the Pawnees."

"How did you and Jake get hooked up?" I asked.

"After my mother died, a missionary took me to live with him and his wife in Omaha, then he moved to Cheyenne. I was in the public schools for six years and I don't think anybody took me for a 'breed. Four years ago the missionary's wife died and I didn't think it would look right for him to keep me. He knew Jake and asked Jake if he wanted a housekeeper and Jake said he did, so I came along with him. We've lived here for four years."

The whole thing made me sore. It was a sweet arrangement for Jake. The missionary knew damned well what being Jake's housekeeper amounted to, but he apparently hadn't said a word about Jake's marrying Ellie. All he wanted was to get the girl off his hands. Chances are he'd taken her in just to be a cheap servant. Even as a child, Ellie was the kind who would do a lot of work for him and not cost him much.

It stacked up like a stinking deal all around to me, and I began to think a little less of Jake Murdock. I knew right away that I was jumping to some conclusions about him. He was doing what other men did in this part of the country and nobody thought anything about it.

Even if Jake did take Ellie for granted, he treated her as well or better than most men treated their wives. He never beat her or cussed her, and I knew for a fact that some men were meaner to their squaws than to their dogs and horses.

"I don't suppose you'd want to go back on the reservation," I said.

"Of course I wouldn't." She folded the pants and laid them on her lap. "I'd kill myself first. Anything would be better than that. But Jake wouldn't send me back." She rose. "I'd better get supper started. The only time Jake gets ornery is when he's hungry and there's nothing to eat."

"How'd your brother get here?" I asked. "Did the missionary take him in, too?"

"Oh, no, he wouldn't have done that," she said, and for the first time there was a hint of bitterness in her voice. "Charley's got a dark skin and Mister Peabody, that was the missionary's name, never let on that I was part Indian. Charley's two years older than I am and he doesn't like it on the reservation any more than I do. He was with a band of Sioux that rode through here a few months after I first came to live with Jake. Charley recognized me, but he'd grown up so much I didn't know him. He stayed here a while and worked for Jake, then he went over to the Rand Ranch and he's been working for Carl Rand ever since."

She built up the fire and came back to where I sat smoking by the window. "Why don't you stay here and work for us, Bill? Jake usually hires a man during the summer. It would be better for you than being a gunman."

"I'll think about it," I said.

I hadn't looked ahead. I knew I'd be able to ride in a few days and I had expected to buy a horse from Murdock and drift on. I had plenty of money, and as far as work was concerned I knew that a man with my talents could always find some kind of a job. But now I began to give her suggestion some thought.

If Ellie had been Mrs. Murdock, I don't think I would have considered staying here for a minute. I never have been much of a hand for hard work and Jake Murdock looked like a slave driver to me, but being cooped up inside this room with Ellie for a week had done something to me.

I wasn't ready to admit it to myself, but the truth was I liked the idea of being around her. It looked to me as if Jake Murdock didn't intend to marry Ellie, and that sooner or later he'd try to send her back to the reservation the way other men of the country were doing. I wanted to be here when that happened.

Murdock came in after a while. All of a sudden I had an impulse to ask him right out plain why he hadn't married Ellie, but I didn't. Hell, you can't ask a man why he doesn't marry the woman he's been sleeping with. Besides, I liked it better the way it was.

Chapter Five

I began to exercise the following week, going outside and walking a little bit each day, and doing a few chores for Ellie such as cutting wood and pumping water. By the end of the week I was thinking about riding, but I had been around Murdock's barn and corral, and I hadn't seen any of his animals I wanted.

"I've got to have a horse," I told him one evening after supper. "Do you know where I can buy one? I want a good, young gelding. When a man buys a horse, I don't think it's the right place to try to save money."

He looked at me approvingly. "You're right," he said. "Yes, I've got just the horse for you."

I shook my head at him. "I've been looking your horses over and I haven't seen one of them I'd give you ten dollars for."

He grinned. "You haven't seen this one. I'll fetch him in tomorrow night, but he'll cost you a hundred dollars."

I'd never been a man to worry about money. I figured I had plenty in my money belt to keep me going until I found work. As long as I lived here, I wasn't out anything and I thought I'd stay a while if Murdock could find something for me to do. I didn't aim to ask for any wages because I owed him plenty. Ellie, too, for taking care of me.

Still, it jolted me a little when he said one hundred dollars. I'd won that amount in the few hands of poker I'd played in Cheyenne, so if I spent it for a horse, I'd still have as much in my money belt as I'd had when I'd hit town. I figured I could go to Cheyenne and have my pick of any horse in town for one hundred dollars, so it wasn't a question of what I'd pay for a horse. The proposition was a matter of getting the best horse I could find.

"I'll have to see him," I said finally.

"Why, sure," he said as if it were a stupid remark, which it was. "I wouldn't expect you to buy a horse sight unseen even on my say so, but this is a good animal. You want to remember one thing. With so many men heading for the Black Hills, horses are in demand. Prices are up and it's hard to buy a good saddle horse."

"I hadn't thought about that," I admitted.

The following evening Murdock rode in leading a sorrel gelding. I hobbled out to the corral as fast as I could. Ellie, who followed me, gasped when she saw the horse. I asked: "What's the matter? Anything wrong with him?"

"Oh, no," she said. "He's a good horse. A fine horse."

He was, too. It was a case of love at first sight. I patted him on the neck and he nuzzled me and that was it. I judged he was probably a four-year-old, a leggy animal with a good chest. I couldn't guess whether he was a stayer or not, but I figured there wasn't any doubt about his being fast.

"I'd like to ride him," I said.

"I'll get your saddle," Murdock said.

He brought my saddle from the barn. I tightened the cinch and mounted. My leg was still weak, but I managed to hoist myself aboard. If the sorrel had been a bucker, I'd have been eating dust the first jump because I didn't have enough strength left in that leg to stay on him if he'd been of a mind to throw me, but he wasn't. He just took off in a nice, easy gait, and we hadn't gone fifty yards until I knew I had to have him.

I rode for half an hour. When my leg began to ache, I turned back. Murdock was working around the barn. I got down, not sure whether my leg was going to hold me or not, but it did. Murdock off saddled, watching me out of the corner of his eyes.

"Well, what about it?" he asked as he turned the sorrel into the corral.

"He's a good horse," I said. "Let me think about it a little while."

He shrugged his beefy shoulders. "No hurry. I'll keep him if you don't want him. Before the summer's over, I'll get better than one hundred dollars for him."

I limped into the house.

Murdock yelled after me: "Tell Ellie I'll be in for supper in about half an hour!"

"I'll tell her," I said.

When I got inside, Ellie was setting the table. I shut the door, and, when she looked up, I said: "You were surprised when you recognized that horse. If there's something wrong with him, I want to know it before I close the deal with Jake."

She straightened and, turning, looked squarely at me. "There is nothing wrong with that horse. Not as far as I know. I've never ridden him, but I've seen him ridden plenty of times. I don't think there's a faster horse anywhere on the Chug than that sorrel."

"How do you know that?"

"He's been in several races and he's never lost."

"When Jake told me last night he had just the right horse for me, you didn't know what horse he meant, did you?"

"No." She turned back to the stove and started frying several slices of ham.

I said: "Ellie, when you saw the horse tonight, you were shocked. Surprised anyway. I heard you gasp like maybe you didn't expect it to be that sorrel. Now I want to know what surprised you."

I guess I spoke more roughly than I intended, but I was getting irritated because I couldn't make her answer my question. She stood there, watching the ham cook for a good minute. It seemed longer, but I didn't prod her. I waited, and after a while she turned around. She said: "Buy the horse, Bill. He's a good one."

"You still haven't told me what I want to know."

She squeezed her lips together and tears began running down her cheeks. I hadn't seen her cry before. In the days I'd been here, she had been a happy person, never complaining even though she worked hard and it seemed to me she simply wasn't appreciated. I had never heard Murdock say—"Thank you."—or compliment her on anything she did. But now it was plain enough that something was bothering her.

"The horse belonged to my brother, Charley Three Horses," she said. "I don't know how Jake got him, but Jake made some kind of a deal with Charley or he wouldn't have brought him. You go ahead and buy him. You'll never get a better horse."

I didn't press her any more. It was my guess she suspected that Jake had run some kind of a sandy on her brother Charley Three Horses, but she didn't want to know about it. I didn't, either. As soon as Murdock came in, I handed him the one hundred dollars and Murdock wrote out a bill of sale and I owned the horse. I named him Sundown. I rode him every day after that, and by the end of April, I was about as good as I ever was. Ellie was right. I never could have bought a better horse.

We had a few more wet snows. The days and nights turned warmer. I saw a few traces of green in the grass, and the buds of the cottonwoods along the Chug began to swell. More and more miners went by on their way to the Black Hills, and now and then a column of cavalry camped along the river.

I wasn't alone with Ellie much after that. It was just as well, too, because I guess I was in love with her by that time. Anyhow, I didn't trust myself. I was careful not to say anything to her. I'd have been a fool if I had.

I knew that nothing would make her leave Murdock as long as he wanted her. It wouldn't have been right anyway, even if I could have made any headway with her. My conscience was elastic in some areas, but not in this regard. I wasn't going to forget that Jake Murdock had saved my life.

I didn't get the rest of the story about Sundown until one day in May when I was riding with Murdock. I don't know what prompted him to tell me, but for no apparent reason he said in an offhand way: "I bought that sorrel you're riding from Ellie's brother Charley Three Horses. He works for Carl Rand. He's a good man with horses, Charley is. He's got a way of gentling 'em that most men don't have. He never gets mean with 'em."

Murdock laughed, a kind of a short, barking laugh that made me think he wasn't real proud of himself. "These 'breeds are a funny lot. You can handle 'em if you know how, though they'll turn on you sometimes if you ain't careful. Charley will be mad when he finds out I made fifty dollars on the deal."

He shot me a quick glance to see how I liked it, then he shrugged his shoulders and stared straight ahead, and that was the end of it. I never heard another word from him about it.

But the thing was Murdock had taken advantage of Charley Three Horses to make a measly fifty dollars, and Ellie must have guessed it or she wouldn't have cried that evening. Maybe Murdock lied to Charley about why he wanted the sorrel. I didn't know, of course, and Ellie didn't tell me if she knew.

Anyhow, Murdock told me a hell of a lot about himself and his attitude toward Ellie and Charley when he said you can handle the half-breeds if you know how. I thought a little bit less of Jake Murdock after he said that.

Chapter Six

I rode every day with Murdock, most of the time from sunup to sundown. On occasion we'd get as far north as the Platte and south almost to Cheyenne. I figured out that he hadn't gone very far south before on account of the Flynns, but now that he had practically wiped them out, he wasn't worried about them.

We rode to the Nebraska line on the east and into the foothills of the Laramie range on the west. We didn't cross any Indian tracks, and that surprised Murdock because small bands had been going back and forth across this country ever since he had settled on the Chug.

He had never been attacked, and he wasn't even sure the Sioux had stolen any of his cattle or horses. He was more inclined to believe that the Flynns had been responsible for anything he had lost.

Murdock insisted that the Sioux had let him alone because he lived with one of their squaws. I doubted that he was right about that. It didn't seem likely they would consider Ellie one of them, even though she had lived with them as a child. The hard truth was half-breeds were often caught between the whites on one hand and the Indians on the other, so they tended to cling to each other and live in a world of their own. Ellie didn't look like a half-breed and could have passed as a white somewhere if she wasn't known as a half-breed. But I understood how it was on the Chug. She would be known as a half-breed as long as she lived here.

Murdock said he was doing all of this riding to look for strays. He'd lost a number of strays that might be due to theft or the winter, but again they might have drifted off his range. At least that was what he said, although as a matter of fact we never did find a stray. What he was really looking for were unbranded calves. When he found one, he stopped, built a fire, heated the JM iron he carried on his saddle, and added another calf to the JM herd. I don't think he ever altered a brand, but I think he would have, if he could have figured out a way to do it and keep his neck out of a noose.

Ranches were few and far between and no one ever did catch Murdock in the act of branding a calf that wasn't his. I don't know what he would have done if one of his neighbors had caught him red-handed, but chances were it would have ended up in a gunfight. He seemed glad to have me along, for protection, I suppose. He claimed he wasn't very good with a gun and he allowed I was.

All the outfits I'd been hooked up with had stolen land. I don't know much about the morals involved. I guess there really isn't a great deal of difference between stealing a quarter-section of land than a calf except that stealing land is a bigger operation. Usually the courts are on the side of the big outfits, and more often than not the sheriff's office goes along. The result is that you're reasonably sure if you're stealing land. On the other hand, if you're caught branding another man's calf, you're going to jail because the sheriff's got the deadwood on you.

It's a cinch you're not part of a big outfit or you wouldn't get involved in a piddling operation, so you've got no protection. The sheriff arrests you, you go to jail, and the judge will send you to the pen, providing you live long enough to go jail. The way I had always viewed it, I guess it was a hell of a lot bigger crime to steal a calf than a quarter-section of land. I'll admit I was pretty uneasy every time Murdock did it. No one caught us, but if somebody had made a count, he would have been amazed at how many of the JM cows had had twins that spring.

I hadn't ridden with Murdock very long until I knew exactly what Ellie meant when she said he had a one-track mind. He wanted a big outfit. I'm not sure why unless it was that his ambition was to be an important man, and a big spread meant money and money meant power. Wyoming was bound to be a state before long, and Murdock could see himself sitting in the governor's chair in Cheyenne or going back to Washington to serve in the United States Senate.

At least once during the day I could count on Murdock's saying: "By God, I've got to get hold of some money. Big money to buy enough cows to hold all the range I'm claiming." Or maybe it would be: "If I had the money, I'd put in a ditch system and take the water out of the Chug over yonder, and I'd have the best damned meadows in Wyoming." One time he looked right at me and he said: "Bill, how'd you like to come in as a half partner in the JM? All it'd take is fifty thousand dollars. That'd buy the herd I need and we would be living like kings in three, four years."

I stared at him for a while, wondering if he had gone loco to think I had $50,000. I said: "Jake, if I had that kind of money, I'd be living like a king right now instead of riding around all day with you helping you steal calves."

That didn't ruffle him a bit, although he did look a little crestfallen. "Yeah, I suppose you would," he said. "The trouble is that even with a good calf crop and good luck stealing calves, it's just gonna take too long. How much money have you got?"

"About five hundred dollars," I answered.

He groaned. "Oh, hell! That wouldn't do much good even if you did throw it into the pot. I've got a thousand buried in the cabin. I've been thinking that as soon as we brand my calves, I'd ride over into Nebraska and pick up as many cows as I could buy with the money I've got. I keep hoping that something will happen that'll drop a pile of *dinero* into my lap. It's gonna happen one of these days. The only question is when."

I had never seen anybody live on dreams day after day the way Murdock did. I'd never placed a very high valuation on money, not wanting to be either rich or important, but I'd been hard-headed about it, too, figuring that whatever a man got, he had to earn in one way or another. It tickled me, but it made me sad, too, that a man like Jake Murdock who was practical in most ways could actually believe that, if he hoped for something long enough and hard enough, it would come to pass.

Maybe he prayed for it, too, although he wasn't a religious man in the usual way you think of a man being religious. He'd say that it couldn't do any harm and it might do some good. The funny part of it was that eventually he got what he wanted, but it didn't come in the way anyone could foresee.

"Why don't you go to Cheyenne and see what some of the bankers will do for you?" I asked. "I'll bet you can find one who'll give you a big enough loan to buy a good-size herd."

He shook his head. "I'll never let a banker get his hooks into me. I like everybody in the world but bankers, and I hate every one of the sons-of-bitches. They ruined my pa. He mortgaged his farm in Missouri to one of 'em, and, as soon as he could, he took it."

"Well, then," I said, "take your thousand and go to Cheyenne and sit in on a poker game. I won a hundred in three hands. You might hit a lucky streak and triple it."

"Or lose all of it." He shook his head at me. "Oh, no. I don't mind gambling on the weather or on the price of beef. Any cowman has to do that, but I'll be damned if I'll gamble on cards."

He was smart at that, I thought. I'd seen men who were driven by an ambition as hard as he was driven by his hunger to own a big spread. Because they couldn't find a better way, they'd try cards and end up losing their shirts. It isn't so bad if you're playing with men who had about the same skill you have, but sooner or later you'll hit a professional. The tin-horn will take the average cowboy in one way or another every crack.

By the time we got into the last of May we were having our share of spring weather, part of the time anyhow. The trees were leafed out and the hills had turned green. Ellie's hens were cackling every day as if laying an egg was a great accomplishment. Murdock's spotted sow had a litter of six pigs and Ellie's black cat had three kittens that were as black as the mother was.

"I didn't think there was a tomcat in a hundred miles of here," Murdock said, "but when the time came, by God, they showed up by the dozen, caterwauling and fighting and raising hell. I don't know how they got the word, but they got it."

Ellie was feeling good these days. She was smiling most of the time and humming those funny little tunes of hers. She had me hook up the team and plow her garden, and, if she could catch me when I wasn't riding with Murdock, she'd get me out there with a hoe and a rake working the big clods down into little clods and then helping her plant.

Murdock would eat what she raised, all right, but he figured working in the garden wasn't a man's business. I figured the same, but after all Ellie had done for me, I didn't have the gall to tell her I wouldn't do her plowing, although it had been a long time since I'd had hold of a pair of plow handles.

One thing was sure. By this time I knew Jake Murdock as well as I ever knew any man in my life. In snatches now and then he told me about his boyhood in Missouri and how that, after his pa lost the farm, they almost starved to death.

The Panic of 1857 was what made it so bad. I was only two years old when it hit, so I didn't remember anything about it except a few things my folks had told me, but according to Murdock it was about as bad as the last one in 1873, and I didn't have any trouble remembering that one.

When we were coming home late one afternoon, we stopped on top of the cliff where Murdock had stood the day he had almost wiped out the Flynns and saved my life. It was the first time we'd been there together, and he told me exactly how it had been and where he was when he'd spotted me and then the Flynns. I was more convinced than ever that he would never have taken a hand in that fight if he hadn't hated the Flynns so much, but that didn't change the facts. He'd saved my life and I wasn't one to forget it.

He was silent quite a while, sitting his saddle there on the cliff and staring off toward the Chug. He said thoughtfully: "My pa was always one to show off and make something look exciting when it wasn't. You've seen men like that, Bill. They've got to be the Big One no matter whether they're hunting rabbits or grizzlies. The trouble with Pa was that he was always hunting rabbits. Ma was the solid one, or we'd have starved to death, I reckon. Anyhow, she was always accusing Pa of what she called bravado. You know what it means?"

"No." I shook my head. "I don't think I ever heard of the word."

"I don't know where she heard it," Murdock said, "but she liked to use it. I don't know exactly what it means, either, but it did seem to fit Pa, at least the way Ma meant it. I reckon it's all right to make a big show of something as long as you really do what you're pretending to do, but Pa was a bag of wind. He lived that way and he died that way. He joined the Union Army and he came home in his blue uniform talking big about how he'd personally save the Union, but he died of a heart attack before he ever cracked a cap. Scared to death, I figure."

Murdock turned his horse around and we rode down off the cliff. We didn't say a word until we got home. Then, as we were stripping gear off our horses, he said: "I've always been afraid I'd end up like Pa, just a bag of wind. Ma's dead, and the chances are she's sitting up there on that big white cloud watching me and telling some other angel she did the best she could for me, but I'm a chip off the old block, all bravado."

"Well, all I can say is you shoot damned straight," I told him.

For the moment at least that seemed to satisfy him.

Chapter Seven

Something happened near the end of May that changed both my life and Murdock's. Ellie's, too, for that matter. It was entirely unexpected, and neither Murdock nor I foresaw what would come out of a more or less routine act. But how could we? It would have taken the seventh son of a seventh son to have foreseen what was going to happen in the next four or five months.

Murdock and I had just returned from a long ride into the foothills of the Laramie range when we saw that a company of cavalry had camped on the Chugwater. Miners on their way to the Black Hills had gone past by the hundreds the last few weeks. Several companies of soldiers bound for Fort Laramie had marched by. When they camped on the Chug, Murdock and I would go to the river and talk to some of the officers, mostly to pick up any gossip we could as to what was happening. It had been plain enough all spring that something big was in the wind.

Hundreds of supply wagons had rumbled past, too. After seeing them and hearing the rumors from the officers we talked to, we figured out a big campaign was being launched to crush the Sioux and Cheyennes. This was typical government maneuvering, of course. Murdock knew more about it than I did because he had lived here all the time, and I'd been on the Picketwire until about two months ago. What had happened was an old story. The Black Hills were supposed to belong to the Sioux, forever, I guess, and maybe they would have if gold hadn't been discovered in them. That was an old story, too. All you've got to do is to whisper gold and you start an epidemic of rushitis.

Anyhow, the government used the Army to try to keep miners out of the Black Hills, but it might as well have tried to hold back the wind. Then Uncle Sam tried to buy the Black Hills, but the Sioux wouldn't sell. They had the law on their side, if you want to call it a law. After that the government had to be sneaky about taking the Black Hills.

If you pretend you're keeping inside the law, the average John Doe jumps on the bandwagon and believes the editorials and land boomers and the politicians and the merchants. The editor sells more newspapers, the land boomer sells more land, the merchant sells more supplies, the politician gets elected to a higher office, and the miner finds gold. Everybody's happy except the Indian, and who the hell cares about the Indian?

What had happened during the winter was that Indians were given until January 31st to move to a reservation, or be turned over to the Army, and, of course, they would be considered hostiles if they didn't come in whether they were or not. This was fine with the Army because it gave the soldiers a chance to fight. That means the officers might get promoted, and naturally they are not going to get promoted lying in bed with their wives on frosty spring mornings.

The Indians were roaming around somewhere on the Powder or the Yellowstone or the Rosebud. It didn't make much difference where they were because they couldn't possibly have come in, with travel as difficult as it is during the wintertime. The truth was the Sioux were given an ultimatum with which it was impossible to comply, and the government knew it.

The proposition was that Uncle Sam had to have an excuse to start a war so the Sioux could be crushed and forced back inside the limited boundaries of a reservation. A new treaty would be jammed down the throats of the Indians and they'd end up signing over the Black Hills to the whites. That way the miners could be let alone and everybody would be happy about the situation except the Indians and the few whites who sympathized with the Indians. I can tell you there were mighty few of those who lived in Wyoming.

I'd admit I was prejudiced because I'd had the story from Murdock and Murdock was prejudiced because he was living with Ellie and he figured he was a good friend of Charley Three Horses. Besides, there used to be roving bands of Sioux that stopped at the JM. Murdock got to know some of them and speak their language a little and trade a few horses. He was a sharp trader and I never knew him to lose on a deal.

We rode down to the Chug to visit with the officers of the cavalry company we saw camped there. It turned out to be Company E, 3rd Cavalry, which was riding as an escort for Colonel W.B. Royall, commanding.

Murdock knew a good many officers because he'd been to Fort Laramie many times and Fort Fetterman a few times, and even to Fort D.A. Russell near Cheyenne occasionally. He'd sell a horse or a shirt tail full of cows or maybe sign a contract to supply wood or hay to one of the posts. He had a flair for making money on deals like that, and I guessed that the $1000 he had buried in his cabin was from this kind of business.

I hadn't met any of the officers who were stationed in Wyoming. Murdock had but he didn't know Colonel Royall. Some officers just naturally look the part and give the appearance of having been born to do exactly what they were doing. The minute you shook hands with Royall, you knew he had all the qualities a cavalry officer needs.

He was about fifty, I judge. He was a tall, very handsome man who stood with a soldier's erect posture. He had a gray mustache and dark brows that shaded a pair of sharp blue eyes. His hair was cropped short and at the top of what seemed to be a very high forehead was a scar. I later learned that, although he was a Virginian, he had fought as a Union soldier in the war and had been slashed by a Confederate saber near Richmond.

We shook hands with Royall and several other officers and met a newspaper reporter named Finerty from Chicago, a cocky little man who smoked a pipe and wore a derby and whose manner assured us he was going to get a story out of this fight whether anyone else did or not. We stood talking to Royall for five or ten minutes. He told us that General George Crook who would command this expedition was at Fort Fetterman; that would be the jumping-off place. The men who had moved north from Fort D.A. Russell made up one wing of the command. Most of them had gone by two days before. The other wing was moving north from Medicine Bow, which was west of Cheyenne on the Union Pacific.

Anyhow, Royall seemed to favor Murdock. He said suddenly: "General Crook needs more scouts than he has. He pays well. If you could make arrangements to have someone take care of your ranch, you might find it worthwhile to sign up with him."

The idea jolted Murdock. He said: "Why, hell, Colonel, I don't know that country. I've never been north of Fort Fetterman in my life."

Royall shrugged as if that were of little concern. "He's got men who know the country. Frank Grouard, for instance, can draw a map of it with his eyes closed. What the general needs is a number of solid men who can act as scouts and who can fight when necessary." He paused, glancing at the soldiers who were strung out along the creek, then added: "Who can travel light and who won't be surprised."

He was an unusual man, this Colonel Royall. He didn't come right out and say it, but it was plain enough that he knew the Army was slowed up with too much materiel and tied by red tape and had too many officers who couldn't think on the spur of the moment. Even the cavalry was not as flexible as it should be; perhaps a body of scouts would be.

Soldiers might be surprised and panicked into stampeding to the rear. It's happened often enough. A sizeable body of tough plainsmen wouldn't be. At least that was the way I interpreted his thinking, and later I learned that Murdock figured the same.

Murdock stood there about half a minute and didn't say a word, but his forehead was all wrinkled up. I could see he was turning this over in his head. After a while he said: "We'll think on it."

He turned to his roan and stepped up.

Royall said: "Don't think on it too long. The general will be taking his command out of Fort Fetterman in a few days. Not more than a week, I'd say."

"We'll decide in a day or two," he said. "Come on, Bill."

He rode toward the house. I mounted and caught up with him. I was amused and a little sore, too, about his use of the word we. He was taking too much for granted. *We* hadn't talked about how long I'd stay.

At first I'd stayed because I knew I had to get my strength back, and after that I'd stayed because I didn't have any plans and I enjoyed riding with Murdock. Later on we'd planned to put up some hay and cut the winter's supply of wood and maybe a few posts, but so far we hadn't really put in a day's work.

Part of the reason for putting off the work we'd talked about was Murdock's distaste for it. He was a cowman and he enjoyed riding chores or branding and cutting calves and breaking horses, but when it came to digging ditches and irrigating fields and putting up hay, he'd postpone it just as long as he could. Maybe this was one reason he considered scouting for Crook.

I'd stayed, too, because I loved Ellie. She was a fine, sweet woman, and the more I saw of her and the longer I stayed, the more sympathy I had for her. Maybe Murdock loved her. I mean, as much as he could love a woman. The truth was he just didn't have room in his head, or heart, either, for anything but his scheming about somehow making a big outfit out of the JM.

If I'd asked Murdock if he loved Ellie, he'd have said, of course he did, and he would have been surprised that I asked. He'd have said: *What do you suppose I brought her here for in the first place?*

I could think of several reasons why he'd brought her to the JM. He needed a housekeeper and he wanted a woman to sleep with, and Ellie was good at supplying both needs. But I didn't spell it out.

One of the first things I had noticed about Murdock was the absolute lack of visible signs of affection on his part. If Ellie did something to indicate she liked him, such as trying to hold his hand or drop an arm around his shoulder, he'd push her away as if he wanted no part of her. I'm not sure that my feeling about Ellie had come completely clear by this time or not, but I had a notion that, if Murdock didn't want Ellie, I did.

I didn't say a word for a while as we rode back to the house. I kept turning it over in my mind, asking myself why he'd said we, and I finally decided to ask him when all of a sudden he made a wide, swinging gesture with his right arm as if he were including the whole country.

"Bill, do you know that by fall, or next summer at the latest, there'll be cattle all over these hills and my chance of having a big spread will be gone? The only thing that's kept this range for us little fry is the Indians who have been raiding all over this part of Wyoming."

I nodded. "I guess that's right. Jake, why did you say we'll think about it and we'll decide?"

He looked at me as if he were shocked. "Why, damn it, I . . . I just thought you were going to stay here. I mean, that we were going to hang together. I wouldn't consider scouting for Crook unless he pays us good money." He stared at me as he scratched his big chin, then he blurted: "Have you got something better to do or somewhere else to go? A girl maybe waiting for you? A family of some kind?"

I shook my head. "Nobody, but . . ."

"All right," he said as if he'd made his point. "It's time you put your roots down and did something besides hiring your gun out to somebody you don't give a damn about. That's no way to live."

He was right about that. I'd had plenty of time to think, lying on that bunk in his big room and staring at the ceiling and my leg hurting so much I couldn't sleep. I'd decided I was going to be something different than a gunfighter, but I hadn't figured on staying here.

"Yeah, I reckon so," I agreed, "but . . ."

"Let's hear no more about it, then," he said. "This is a big country. Plenty of chance for both of us to get ahead. All we need is more money. It takes money to make money."

I didn't argue any more. I figured he was right. I'd come back with my pockets bulging. After the campaign was over, well, I'd have plenty of time then to decide.

Chapter Eight

After supper Murdock sat back and stuffed his pipe. He said casually: "I'm going over to see your brother Charley. Bill and me are going to finish branding tomorrow and the day after that we're riding to Fort Fetterman. General Crook is leading a big expedition against the Sioux and we're going to scout for him. That is, if he'll have us and pay us enough to make it worth our time."

Ellie had raised her cup of coffee halfway to her mouth. It froze there. She stared at Murdock as if she couldn't believe what she'd heard. He struck a match and fired his pipe, and then rose.

Ellie whispered: "You don't mean that?" She set her cup back on the table. She said: "Jake, don't do it."

"Why the hell not?" he demanded. "The Sioux ain't your people no more. What are you talking that way for?"

"No, the Sioux aren't my people," she said bitterly. "Neither are the whites. I'm asking you not to go." She swallowed. "You won't come back."

He snorted derisively. "Sure I will. I wouldn't go if I didn't figure it was the best way I can raise some quick money. I've got to buy more cows. It's the only way I can hold my range. I don't suppose I can hold all of it no matter what happens, but I sure aim to hold every acre I can."

He walked out of the room. She sat motionlessly, staring after him, then she whispered: "Don't let him go, Bill."

"Ellie, you've known Jake a lot longer than I have," I said. "Can you remember anybody ever changing his mind once he gets it made up?"

"No," she answered. "I can't. He's a bull-headed man."

She put her head down on her arms and began to cry. It wasn't like her. For a few seconds I didn't know what to do or say. I hadn't been around a crying woman for a long time, and it made me uneasy. I couldn't think of anything that would comfort her, so I got up and went out to the barn.

Murdock had saddled a bay he rode once in a while when he wanted to rest his roan. He mounted just as I came up. I said: "She's crying."

"Damn it," he said irritably. "You never know what a woman's gonna do. What's the matter with her?"

"I didn't think there was any secret about that," I said. "She doesn't want you to go."

"Well, if she thinks she can talk me out of it . . ." He raised a hand and tipped his hat forward over his eyes. "You know, Bill, it looks to me like I'm gonna have to send her back to the reservation."

I shook my head. "You can't do that."

Telling Jake Murdock he couldn't do something

was always a challenge and he bristled every time. He said sharply: "Who says I can't?"

"Nobody says so except Ellie," I said, a little sore now myself at the way he was performing. He knew he was being stupid as well as I did. "She wouldn't go. You heard what she said. You said it yourself. The Sioux aren't her people and they haven't been since she was a child."

He shrugged. "Yeah, the 'breeds have a hard time. They don't fit nowhere. Just with each other. Well, we'll see, but Ellie had better not try telling me what I can or can't do. She knows better."

He rode off then. I didn't want to see Ellie any more after that, so I fiddled around the barn until Murdock got back with Charley Three Horses about dusk. I had never seen Charley, and, although Murdock had told me he had a dark skin, I was surprised he was as dark as he was. He could easily have passed for a full-blooded Sioux.

We shook hands and I said I was glad to meet him. He stood looking at me in the thin light for several seconds, then he said: "You like my horse you bought?"

For a moment I was puzzled, then I remembered that Murdock had bought Sundown from him and had sold him to me. I said: "You bet I do. He's a good horse."

"Good horse." Charley nodded. "I raised him. I broke him to ride."

"You did a good job," I said.

"Charley's the best man in the country when it comes to breaking horses," Murdock said. "Well, I'm going to bed. You sleep in the barn, Charley. After we leave, you can have the bunk in the house where Bill's sleeping now."

I found it hard to believe that he and Ellie were full brother and sister. Of course, you never know how half-breeds are going to fall when they're crossed with whites, and, as I walked back to the house, the thought occurred to me that, if Ellie ever had a baby, he would be only one-eighth Sioux, but he might be as dark as Charley Three Horses.

I didn't know how Ellie would be the next morning, but she was as happy as ever, on the surface at least. She was smiling and humming one of her special tunes when I went back into the house for breakfast. We worked hard all day rounding up Murdock's calves and branding them. It had been like Murdock to ride to hell and gone for weeks trying to find a few unbranded calves so he could slap the JM iron on them, but he'd let his own go until the last minute.

Murdock's cows had stayed close enough to the ranch so I doubt that he lost any calves. We finished by dark. Charley Three Horses was a good hand, one of the best I ever worked with. He handled the irons and did a good job. There wasn't a smudged brand in the bunch.

I had a notion that, if he were given any kind of a chance, he'd do all right for himself, but the odds were he wouldn't have much of a chance. There was a lot of prejudice against half-breeds in this country. About all they could do was to hire out to the Army as scouts, and that was something Charley Three Horses would never do.

I fell into bed the minute I finished eating supper. Ellie was still doing dishes when I dropped off to sleep. When I woke at dawn, she was getting break-fast. I went outside, so stiff and sore from wrestling calves the day before I could hardly move.

When I got to the barn, I found that Murdock was in the same fix. Neither one of us had done much hard work all spring, but Charley Three Horses was as good as ever. He had already fed and watered Sundown and Murdock's roan by the time we reached the corral.

As Charley walked to the house with me, he said: "You been on Powder River?"

I nodded. "Four years ago."

"You find plenty Sioux on Powder River," he said. "Maybe on Tongue River."

I never did learn how he knew that. Maybe he just made a good guess, but he was sure right as Crook found out. We ate breakfast and Ellie gave us each a lunch she had fixed for us. Then, before Murdock could do anything to stop her, she threw her arms around him and kissed him.

I was surprised because she had never done that in front of me before. I guess Murdock was surprised, too, but both of us were even more surprised when she turned to me and hugged and kissed me just as hard as she had Murdock.

I couldn't remember when I had been kissed by a woman before, but even if I had been in the habit of being kissed, this would have been a special one. That was what surprised me the most. I don't know whether she could love two men at the same time or not, or whether she even thought about it, but I had a notion she loved me. I don't think I could have mistaken what her lips told me or the way her arms clung to me. Not that much anyway.

When she finally let me go, she turned and walked to the stove and stood with her back to us. Charley had brought our horses to the front door and was waiting. Ellie didn't move as long as we were in the house. We went outside and mounted. Murdock gave Charley a bare half-inch nod and I raised my hand to him. Charley grunted something that might have been: "So long."

We rode away, Murdock not saying a word until we were a mile or more from the house. He'd keep glancing at me and then he'd look ahead and after a while he'd look at me again. Finally he said: "Bill, judging from the way Ellie kissed you, she's more worried about you not coming back than she is me."

I shook my head. "Not more worried. She's worried about both of us. I know one thing. She wouldn't trade you for me."

He stared straight down the road after that and didn't say a word for half an hour or more. It struck me kind of queer. That was the first time Murdock had given the slightest hint that he was jealous about Ellie.

Chapter Nine

Most of eastern Wyoming bears no resemblance to the Garden of Eden. Much of the country through which we rode after leaving the JM was covered by sagebrush and cactus. We passed a couple of freight outfits bound for Fort Fetterman.

Hoofs and wheels raised such dense clouds of alkaline dust that I thought I'd smother before we got around them. Then my eyes began to burn and water, and I had an idea I'd be blind before we even reached Fort Laramie.

When we arrived at the fort, I washed off most of the dust and felt better than I expected. We had supper and a couple of drinks and learned that General Crook was at Fetterman, which was what Colonel Royall had said and what we expected.

We were on our way again by sunup the next morning, hoofs cracking sharply on the flooring of the long bridge that spanned the North Platte. The bridge had been finished only a short time before, and nearly all the soldiers and supply trains belonging to Crook's expedition crossed here.

A bitter wind was blowing from the east now. There had been a hard rain here not long before and the ground was muddy, which slowed us up. The air was damp, making the wind feel colder than it actually was.

Part of the time we clung to the north bank of the river. On other occasions we stayed on the road, which was some distance from the Platte, so we often traveled for miles without seeing any water except the dirty, stagnant pools that remained after the rain.

The one bright spot as far as scenery was concerned was Laramie Peak, which reared its conical head far above the rest of the range. It was snow-covered and looked very inviting later in the day when the wind died down and the sun hammered at us from a clear sky.

I had never been through this country before. The winter I had spent on the Powder with Burke Teller had been pleasurable, but we'd traveled west of here in the fall when the weather had been practically perfect. Now it seemed to me I had been freezing all morning and roasting all afternoon.

To make it worse, this country was far more barren than that south of Fort Laramie. We rode up and down into sand pits and over hills. I could see no trees of any kind, no grass, no sagebrush or cacti. Just the damned white sand that was blinding with the sun as bright as it was.

To hell with it, I thought. I didn't have to be here. I had made no commitment and I was of a mind to turn back. I wondered why I had ever let Jake Murdock talk me into this.

We reached Crook's camp across the river from Fort Fetterman in the afternoon of May 26th and found that Colonel Royall with his escort, Company E, 3rd Cavalry, had pulled in ahead of us. We had barely arrived in time as we soon learned. General Crook would be leading the entire expedition north the following morning. We were directed to Crook's tent and reported to his aide, telling him who we were and why we had come. The aide scratched on the flap of the tent and we were told to enter.

Crook was seated on a camp chair, a packing crate in front of him serving as a desk. We introduced ourselves, and Crook, who seemed glad to see us, shook hands cordially. He had never met Murdock, although, like many military men who moved back and forth between Forts D.A. Russell on the south and Laramie and Fetterman on the north, he had heard of Murdock. He had not, of course, heard the name Bill Lang. That, I thought, was just as well.

He was in his late forties, I judged. He was an active-appearing man, with none of the barracks fat that a good many officers take on during peacetime. I had a feeling that, if he had participated in an athletic contest with his enlisted men, he would have come out very well.

His hair was cropped short, his beard was blond and seemed to divide naturally in the middle; his eyes were blue-gray. He was a good six feet tall, broad-shouldered, and, as he stood there frankly sizing us up, I was impressed as I had been with Colonel Royall by his erect posture. I was also convinced that, when the shooting started, here was an officer who wouldn't be sitting inside his tent while his men were getting killed.

We looked him over as frankly as he did us, maybe for a good part of a minute, then Murdock said: "We're here to sign on as scouts, but it'll have to pay us enough to make it worthwhile."

"You will receive one hundred and twenty-five dollars a month if we furnish your horse," he said. "If you have your own horse, you'll get one hundred and fifty dollars."

Murdock glanced at me and nodded. I nodded back. We had talked about it on the way and decided he'd probably offer us one hundred dollars a month. We'd take it if he did, so we were well satisfied to receive half again as much as we had expected.

"Good," Murdock said. "We're your men. We both have good horses."

"You know the country north of here?" Crook asked. "I'd better tell you I can't put a boundary on what that country will be. We'll go anywhere we have to in order to drive the Sioux back onto the reservation, but it will certainly be in the Powder River country or perhaps on the Tongue. We may get as far north as the Yellowstone."

Murdock shook his head. "I've never been north of Fetterman."

"It doesn't make any difference," Crook said quickly. "I have several scouts who know the country as well as most of us know our back yards. We will also pick up some Shoshone and Crow scouts in a few days."

Murdock had said he didn't know the country north of Fetterman, and that was true, but I did, and

I could see that Crook was taking Murdock's word for both of us. That was the way Murdock wanted it. I could play second fiddle to him, but Jake Murdock didn't play second fiddle to anyone. He had turned and started to leave the tent, then stopped and swung around to see what was keeping me.

It had occurred to me that it was time I started speaking up for myself, so I said: "Sir, I spent a winter on the Powder four years ago with an old mountain man named Burke Teller. We got as far west as the Big Horns, but we never crossed them."

Crook's sharp eyes were pinned on my face. He said: "I never met Burke Teller, but I've heard a great deal about him. I understand that he had an uncanny memory of any country he had seen once and he could draw an accurate map of it."

"Yes, sir," I said, "he could do that. I can't, but we did some trapping and hunting and a little trading with several bands of Indians we ran into, so I've been over the country between the Belle Fourche and the Tongue several times."

"That's interesting," Crook said. "Now tell me something. If you were alone and traveling at night and knowing that you might run into a band of hostiles between here and our camp, do you think you could get through?"

"Yes, sir," I answered. "You can't learn everything a man like Burke Teller knows in one winter. At least I couldn't, but when your life and your scalp depends on your learning just to keep from dying, you find that it's quite a bit."

Crook nodded as if he understood that. He asked: "How much do you weigh?"

"One hundred fifty pounds."

"Do you own a good horse? By good horse, I mean one that can take a stiff pace and hold it."

"Yes, sir." I hadn't figured out what he was getting at, but I had a hunch it might be something I wanted and I was going to play it for all it was worth. "He's a sorrel, four years old I think. I've only owned him about six weeks, so I haven't had an opportunity to test him out, but I know he's fast, and I think he'll hold up."

"Well, now," Crook said, "I don't know anything about you, but this is a situation where you either come through or you're a dead man. I'm sure you can be trusted to do what you're told or you wouldn't be with Jake Murdock."

He shot a glance at Murdock, and then went on: "I need a courier who can shuttle back and forth carrying dispatches between my command and the fort which has the nearest telegraph station. The Army will pay you two hundred dollars for each trip you make. If you show you can do it, the war correspondents will more than likely want you to carry some of their stories and put them on the wire. Are you interested?"

"I want the job," I said, thinking that any way I looked at it, I'd be further ahead financially than if I simply rode with the scouts.

"Now you'd better think it over," Crook said. "It's a very dangerous assignment. You'll be on your own. You'll live or die by your wits and what Burke Teller taught you. On what your horse can do, too, of course."

"I want the job," I said again.

Crook smiled. "Very well. We'll try you. You'll ride with the scouts until I need a courier."

I walked out of the tent with Murdock who was staring at me with a sour-tempered expression on his broad face I had seldom seen there. He said: "Well, by God, you got yourself a courier job."

"Looks like it," I agreed.

"I heard what he said about trusting you because you were with me," Murdock said.

He was sullen. All of a sudden it struck me he was acting like a spoiled kid who had lost a plum he had found desirable. The last thing I wanted was to quarrel with him, so I said: "I owe the job to you."

That was all it took. He said: "Yeah, I figured you did."

Five minutes later he was as good-natured as ever. I kept asking myself why Crook picked me for this job when he had other men he knew far more about than he did me. About the time I dropped off to sleep that night the answer came to me. He didn't want to lose any of the others.

It was not a comforting thought.

Chapter Ten

The Big Horn and Yellowstone Expedition, as Crook's command was called, camped on the flat north of the Platte. Fort Fetterman was located on a bluff directly south of our camp. Neither Murdock nor I made any effort to cross the swollen stream in the ferryboat that was available. There was no point in it. As a matter of fact, some of the correspondents who had to get to the telegraph office at the fort were almost drowned making the crossing.

Murdock and I found the body of scouts and camped with them. Some were men like us who were here because they wanted work and were familiar enough with this kind of life to be counted on when the chips were down. Others were experts on the country and the habits of the Sioux. Crook naturally would depend on these men for advice and information about the terrain ahead of us, particularly Frank Grouard, Baptiste Pourier, and Louis Richaud.

A good many of the scouts were whites, but there

were a number of half-breeds, too, most of them as dark as Charley Three Horses, and so could have passed as full-blooded Sioux. Crook had about one hundred wagons carrying supplies, but he also took a pack train of 295 mules.

Crook had had a good deal of experience against the Apaches in Arizona, and, although campaigning against the Sioux was a lot different from fighting the Apaches, he was a practical man who had learned one thing that a good many officers never did learn. That was the simple fact that he could take mules anywhere he had to go, but there were plenty of places where a wagon couldn't go.

A large percentage of the packers were half-breeds, and we soon had some ugly rumors floating around among the soldiers that the half-breeds would sell us out when the shooting started because they were related to the Sioux and we'd have the packers fighting us from the rear while Sitting Bull and his warriors were hitting us in front.

We didn't know for sure that Sitting Bull would be leading the Sioux, but he was the man who had received the most publicity, so it was natural that all of us, including the correspondents, gave him the credit. At the time not much was known of Crazy Horse. Although there was nothing to those rumors about the packers, it was disconcerting to hear them.

We were on the move early on the morning of May 29th, fifteen troops of cavalry and five companies of infantry. This added up to 1,002 men and forty-seven officers. The foot soldiers took the lead, followed by the wagons, then the pack mules, and finally the cavalry in columns of twos.

The scouts naturally were far up ahead. When we

were nearly at the top of the long ridge that lifted to the north, I hipped around in the saddle and looked back. It was quite a sight, and one that I never forgot as long as I lived.

The expedition made a line about four miles long. I could see some of the buildings of the fort above the Platte, and the last of the cavalry leaving the campground at the base of the bluff on our side of the river. The white tops of the wagons were tipping back and forth so that it took very little imagination on my part to think of them as sailing ships on a rough sea, the comparison that is so often made of them. Over all of it was the everlasting dust, and I was thankful I was a scout and not a horse soldier or a "walk-a-heap" as the Indians called the infantryman.

I felt sorry for the Sioux. This was a big outfit, perhaps the biggest expedition that ever took the field against the Indians. At the time I personally knew almost nothing about Sitting Bull or Crazy Horse or any of the Sioux war chiefs. If I had, I wouldn't have felt sorry for the Sioux. Maybe for us, but not the Sioux.

That was the way it was for days as we followed the old Bozeman Trail north or a little west of north. Slowly the miles piled up behind us. Hot days and cold days, wind that burned our skin and cracked our lips, dust that worked into our clothes and our hair and into our food so it gritted between our teeth as we ate.

New sights, new smells of dust, of unwashed bodies, of horse nitrogen. Slowly hour after hour we crawled toward the Powder. Sometimes Murdock would look at me and shake his head and ask why in hell wasn't he back on the JM attending to his business as a rancher. Then he'd say he guessed his mother would say this was just stupid bravado.

I often wondered about this because Murdock sometimes mentioned the JM, and, even when he didn't, it was plain enough that only one thing was important in his life: He had to make his ranch the biggest outfit on the Chug. Sometimes I think he would have robbed a bank to have raised the money he needed to build the spread he dreamed about if he had been certain he wouldn't have been caught.

We reached the site of old Fort Reno on June 2nd. Apparently Crook expected to find a band of Crow warriors waiting, but they were nowhere in sight. The fort had been destroyed years before, and now we found nothing except the remnants of walls and partly burned timbers and pieces of rusty iron scattered on the ground.

Crook called me to his tent that night and started me back to Fort Fetterman with his dispatches and the stories written by the war correspondents who were with the expedition. He even rode to the edge of the camp, giving me advice about how to avoid being caught by Indians. I didn't need it. I didn't consider myself an expert plainsman, but I had learned more from Burke Teller than General Crook knew. It all came back to me once I was riding south and I knew that I was entirely on my own.

I made it to the fort without incident, delivered the dispatches and news stories, and picked up everything that had come in for Crook, but coming back was a different story. I reached the Powder, all right, and found our old campground. I rode at night, and so far I had not sensed the presence of any Indians.

Burke Teller used to say he guessed he was like a mule or a dog that could sense the presence of Indians when he couldn't see them. I always figured he smelled them, but on this occasion I had a little better idea how it was.

I had camped on the west bank of the Powder with a thick screen of willows all around me except on the river side. I had pulled the saddle off Sundown and had left him back in the brush so he couldn't be seen unless someone passed within ten feet of him.

I woke about noon, not sure what woke me except that the sun was hot and squarely over my head. There was something else I couldn't exactly identify, a vague uneasiness that made me move slowly and carefully.

I started to get up to move back into the willows so I would be in the shade, and that was when I suddenly became aware of a band of Sioux warriors riding down the opposite bank to water their horses.

If I had stood up or made a quick move of any kind, I would have attracted the Indians' attention. I didn't count them, but there must have been a dozen or more braves in the band, young bucks painted up and looking for trouble.

I've been scared plenty of times. The first gunfight when I had to face a man in the street, for instance. I knew that a split second difference in our draws meant life or death for me. It scared me so badly that I didn't sleep much for a week afterwards.

This was something else. I couldn't fight. In the first place, Crook had ordered me to avoid a fight. He told me that he wasn't sending me to Fetterman to kill Indians. In the second place, I wouldn't have had the slightest chance against that many braves looking for a scalp. The best I could hope for was that they wouldn't see me.

My scalp began to tingle and prickles worked up and down my spine, and then I had a weird sensation of thinking a million crawling things were moving all over me. But I didn't panic and that was what saved my life.

I eased slowly back into the willows, moving on my belly until I was out of their sight. When I got to Sundown, I put my hand over his nose so he wouldn't nicker and I stood there, hardly breathing. I bent down a little because I didn't want my head to show above the willows, although I don't think it would have if I'd stood straight up.

In the ten minutes or so that the Sioux warriors stood on the opposite side of the river, drinking and watering their horses and then arguing with each other, I felt as if I aged ten years.

I thought about Murdock and what his mother had called bravado. I decided that taking the courier's job was exactly that and I was a damned fool and I'd better keep on hiring my gun to some crooked rancher who was busting his gut trying to steal more range.

My thoughts didn't change much of anything. I was stuck right there until the Indians moved and I thought they were never going to. They gesticulated and talked and finally got on their ponies and headed across the river straight at me.

My God, they'll find me now for sure. That was the first thought that rushed through my mind. My heart was in my throat for the time it took them to ford the river, and I remembered everything I had heard of the cruel tortures the Sioux gave their prisoners. Well, they weren't taking me prisoner. I decided that as I drew my gun.

For some reason that I have never figured out they began angling downstream and hit the west bank of the Powder about thirty yards below me. They kept going, right on through the willows and up the steep slope, and finally disappeared somewhere to the west. I never saw them again.

It was a long time before I could get a good breath. I didn't sleep any more that day, and I stayed right there in the willows until it was black dark. Then I had a queer feeling when I started out that I had been granted another life, that I had been a dead man, but now I lived again.

I found the command camped on the Tongue. There had been an attack by a small party of Sioux, maybe one hundred warriors, although there was no agreement on the number. It wasn't serious, of course, because that small a party wouldn't stand and fight against an outfit the size of Crook's, but it had created some excitement.

A few shots were fired and Colonel Anson Mills took a squadron of the 3rd Cavalry and drove the Indians off the bluff. Everybody including Murdock was excited about it, and, when they finally got around to asking me about my trip, I said: "No trouble."

I hadn't fired a shot and I hadn't been fired at. I just didn't see any point in saying I'd been scared to death.

Chapter Eleven

Crook moved his camp back eleven miles to Goose Creek. I guess he decided to wait for the Crows and Shoshones to join his command, but it wasn't my lot to sit around camp or fish or make the idiotic jaw-bone bets of $10,000 that some of the men did on foot races. Crook called me to his tent and said I was to head back to Fetterman with more dispatches.

I had reported to the general when I first reached camp, but I hadn't told him how close I'd come to losing my hair on the Powder that day. I told him now, mostly I guess because I wasn't real sure I wanted to make the ride again. A man doesn't get over a scare like that right away, although I didn't forget I had made the rest of the trip to Fetterman without seeing hide nor hair of a hostile, and the chances were good I'd make the ride a dozen more times without seeing any Indians.

Crook sat there, tapping his fingertips on the top of the packing crate that served as a desk, and stared at me. He said:" You want me to look for another courier?"

I shook my head. I don't know why, but for some reason I felt better just telling him. "No." That's all I said, but it satisfied him.

"I am fully aware that there is an excellent chance you'll get killed," he said. "It would not be an easy death. I also have some idea of the thoughts that go through a man's head while he's making a ride like that, alone and a long way from help on either end."

"Yes, sir," I said, "but now that I've made the ride, I think it will be easier next time."

He nodded, smiling a little. "I think it will, Lang. You're no bragger. You're a capable man. I'm confident that you'll get through."

This may sound stupid, but his saying that bolstered my confidence. I thought about it a good deal that trip, how that many of the scouts were braggers. Murdock wasn't exactly a bragger, but he was dead sure of himself. Just like the time he was on top of the cliff when I was running from the Flynns and he held his fire until he was absolutely certain he could cut them down with his Winchester just as effectively as if he'd had a Gatling gun.

Murdock was going to get the money he needed to make the JM the biggest ranch on the Chug, maybe even in all of eastern Wyoming. He didn't know how he was going to get it, but it seemed to me that every day the certainty grew in him that he was going to get it.

I wasn't driven by any long-range goal the way Murdock was. I wasn't like most of the other scouts who had come along for the big money, either. As soon as the campaign was over, they'd light out for

Cheyenne and get drunk and crawl into bed with the first whore they found, and in twenty-four hours they'd be broke again.

Funny about the thoughts that come to a man when he's out there in an empty country all by himself and he knows that each hollow he comes to or any clump of willows he passes may hold an Indian who's waiting to catch him in his sights and knock him off his horse. The dangerous time is early in the morning when it begins to get daylight and you've got to keep riding until you find a place to hole up. If the element of chance brings you head on with a band of Indians, you're a dead man.

You begin to ask questions. I had never been one to think about God, but I did on that ride. Maybe it was the danger that I sensed was all around me, or the sheer immensity of the land that dwarfed me and seemed to be totally empty except for me and the antelope and the coyotes who were calling to each other from some distant rim. Perhaps it was the loneliness. Or the feeling that the land wasn't really empty, that there could be a dozen bands of Indians within ten miles of me and I might not see any of them unless they wanted me to. This, of course, brought my thoughts back to the unseen danger that I felt threatened me, and suddenly the prickles began running up and down my back.

A feeling came to me that seemed to free my thoughts. At least they ran wild and maybe a little crazy because they weren't limited by my ordinary common sense. I got to thinking about the cause of things, that if God had created me, He must have given me some kind of purpose for being here which was more important than carrying General

Crook's dispatches to Fort Fetterman or hiring my gun to some yellow-bellied, miserable coward who was afraid to do his own fighting.

Well, I was done with hiring my gun. As far as carrying dispatches was concerned, the campaign wasn't going to last forever. I'd take advantage of it as long as it did last and fill my money belt. I'd go back to the JM and take Murdock up on his offer of a partnership. Between us maybe we'd have enough money to buy a respectable herd, and we'd hold the range he was afraid he'd lose.

No, it just didn't come out right. I couldn't go on living with Murdock and Ellie, knowing all the time that sooner or later he'd get rid of her and try to send her back to the reservation. He'd never come right out and said it in plain words, but I knew what he'd do sooner or later. He'd want a white woman for a wife, and I figured that was the reason he had kept putting Ellie off, making vague promises about marrying her, and never doing it.

Any way I looked at it, there was going to be hell to pay sooner or later, and I didn't want to be Murdock's partner when the time came. I thought about it all the way to the fort, but I didn't have any answers to my questions when I got there.

I still had some funny feelings. One was that I was looking right down the barrel of life into the future and I knew what was going to happen. Maybe I could help Ellie some way, at least tell her that I loved her, although I knew it might lead to more trouble than it would do good.

I caught up on my sleep when I got to Fetterman, let Sundown rest, then picked up the dispatches and got back to camp without seeing as much as a single Sioux warrior. I had begun to feel I hated Jake Murdock for the way he had treated Ellie and what he was going to do to her, but that wasn't any good. All I could do was to be with Ellie when the breakup came.

As soon as I rode into camp on Goose Creek, I found out that Crook had run into the Sioux on the Rosebud and had taken a beating, and Murdock had been right in the thick of it.

"I heard a few bullets talking to me as they went past," Murdock said. "I never seen so much shooting and riding and yelling in my life, or so much dust being raised. I don't know yet why we didn't lose more men. I don't know why we didn't whip 'em, or why they just rode off 'bout two o'clock. We'd been fighting about six hours and they'd had enough. Frank Grouard says they just got hungry and tired and went home and maybe that's it, but I've got a notion that, if they'd kept at us, they'd have run us right up the Rosebud and cut us to pieces."

He packed his pipe and looked at me out of the corners of his eyes. He lowered his voice as he said: "And another thing. I don't know why the general came back to his base camp here on Goose Creek. I hear we're low on ammunition. Mebbeso, mebbeso, but, by God, we didn't take that much of a beating. We should've gone after 'em."

Later on I heard several stories about the battle. One was that, if it hadn't been for the scouts and the packers and the Crows and the Shoshones who held the Sioux off until the soldiers got organized, it would have been a sad and bloody day on the Rosebud. One thing was sure. Crook found out that fighting the Sioux was a lot different than fighting the Apaches.

It was hard to know what the real truth was. Crook contended the Army won the battle and the Indians were defeated because they withdrew and left the soldiers in possession of the field. That was his way of looking at it, but some of the other officers felt humiliated and said frankly that, since the Indians hadn't been smashed and pursued and scattered, they had won the fight, not the Army.

So you take your choice. In any case, Crook decided to stay right there in camp and send for reinforcements and supplies and ammunition. The wagon train was to return to Fetterman with the wounded, and, as soon as I was rested, I was back in the saddle on Sundown, headed for the fort with Crook's dispatches that included his and other officers' reports of the fight. I had the idea, as Colonel Mills said, that most of them took little pride in their accomplishment.

I was at Fort Fetterman when the news came in about the Custer fight and it was my job to carry dispatches to General Crook telling about the battle, arriving on Goose Creek July 10th. Some of the scouts knew men who were killed on the Little Big Horn, and, of course, many of the officers knew Custer personally as well as others who died there.

It was a grim and depressed camp after the news got around. I suppose that everybody wondered if the tragedy might have been prevented if Crook had moved on down the Rosebud instead of retreating to Goose Creek. There was the other side to it, too. If Crook had gone down the Rosebud, he might have met the same fate Custer did.

I have never been able to understand how an experienced Indian fighter like Custer could lose his life and his five companies of cavalry could be wiped out to a man. This summer of 1876 was different for the Sioux than any other year.

I'm not sure why this was so. Perhaps it was due to the inspiration of Sitting Bull's visions, or Crazy Horse's generalship, or maybe it was the sheer desperation rising from the Black Hills situation that made the Sioux fight with courage and persistence and group action they had never demonstrated before. Whatever the causes, it was certainly a year of change for many of us and the high-water mark for the Sioux.

Along with the other dispatches I carried was a telegram from General Sheridan to Crook that said: *Hit them again and hit them harder.* Crook smiled a little when he read that. He was pretty grim about it, I thought, and didn't have much to say, but he still wasn't in any hurry to resume the campaign. As a matter of fact, he went hunting. I have an idea that the Big Horn Mountains west of Goose Creek were about as near heaven as General George Crook ever found himself in this life.

The Indians were still in the country, their scouting parties keeping an eye on everything the soldiers did, although I never saw any of them again on my rides between camp and Fort Fetterman. Grouard and Pourier and other scouts who fanned out to the north and west found it hard to determine for sure what the hostiles were doing because they set fire to the timber in the mountains and the grass on the plains, making the smoke so heavy it was difficult to observe anything.

In the end the scouts decided that most of the Indians had gone north toward Canada, probably because the game had been pretty well killed off in this part of the country. Crook decided to resume the campaign on August 3rd, giving orders to abandon the tents and rely on the pack train. This, of course, brought an end to my duties as courier.

From then on I rode as a scout, drawing the $150 a month pay that was what Murdock had been drawing. I had sometimes made twice that much for a single round trip to the fort and back, depending on whether I took some of the correspondents' stories or the general's dispatches only, so I was sorry to see my good thing come to an end.

Still, it was pleasant to be riding beside Murdock again, although it took about one minute to find out he hadn't changed a bit. He looked straight at me as if he were a little envious. He said: "I guess you made a lot of money taking those sashays to the fort."

"Yeah, quite a bit," I agreed.

His eyes narrowed and his lips tightened against his front teeth and he said: "Don't forget about that partnership deal we talked about."

"No, I haven't forgotten about it," I said.

I let it go at that. I didn't say a word about Ellie, and I sure didn't mention any of those crazy thoughts I'd had about what I was supposed to be doing with my life. He'd have laughed his damned head off if I had.

Chapter Twelve

Apparently Crook expected General Wesley Merritt to show up sooner than he did, but Merritt had a brush with a band of Cheyennes who had left the Red Cloud Agency apparently headed west to throw in with the hostiles Crook was after. Merritt forced the Cheyennes back to the reservation, then turned west again and joined Crook, but the action did delay him several days.

The command now numbered about 2,000 men. The wagons, 160 of them, were sent back to Fort Fetterman, and orders were given for each man to carry one hundred rounds of ammunition and four days' rations. In addition, the pack train carried fifteen days' rations per man and the extra ammunition.

The situation didn't look good to me or Murdock, either, but Crook neglected to ask our opinion. The horses were in sad shape. Crook's cavalry had had no grain to feed the animals since early in June, and Merritt's horses were about used up after their pursuit of the Cheyennes. Even with the long rides,

Sundown was in about the best shape of any of the horses because he'd been well fed when I was at Fort Fetterman.

I rode with the scouts ahead of the main column, with Frank Grouard and Bill Cody in the lead. Cody had come in with Merritt. Grouard, of course, was the best, but as far as I was concerned Cody was strictly bluff and a big wind. He looked the part of a plainsman, all right, decked out in his buckskin outfit and his big, white hat with the snake band and his brown silky hair falling over his shoulders. The newspapermen were fooled and thought he was the real thing, so they built him up big the way they do, but Murdock and most of the scouts felt the way I did, a little sick way down in their bellies.

We hit some hot weather, the kind that boils the juice right out of a man. It was over one hundred degrees, I think. We'd make twenty or twenty-five miles a day, sometimes through mighty rough country, cliffs and small pines and ridges and very little water. We had to lay over one day because of a combination of fog and smoke that was like a heavy curtain blotting out the earth. A breeze came up that evening about six and cleared the air. The result was that we were in for a night march.

We went down the Rosebud, cavalry on the flanks, infantry and pack train in the middle. The night was as black as sin until the moon rose. The whole thing seemed a weird experience to me, moving through country that not even many of us scouts really knew.

From where I rode, I could hear a mule now and then express himself loudly behind me; I heard the *thud* of the hoofs of the cavalry and the metallic clatter of carbines and sling belts. Occasionally a soldier would strike a match to fire his pipe, the match flame a tiny, brief burst of light in the darkness. At least the Sioux gave us no trouble, and we were thankful for that.

We stopped at two o'clock in the morning to catch a few hours' sleep. The next day we made another twenty miles, but the horses were in worse shape than ever because the Sioux had burned the grass. Those of us who were scouts could do better for our horses because we rode ahead or to one side or other of the column and now and then found side cañons and draws where there was a little grass.

Then a cold rain hit us, a piercing wind from the north driving the rain at us, and the dust was replaced by mud. Of course, we began wishing we had some of the searing heat we'd experienced a few days before. Murdock looked at me and shook his head.

"I've seen some tough weather during roundup," he growled, "but, by God, I never seen none worse than this."

If I hadn't been hungry and so cold I was shivering as if I had chills and fever, I'd have laughed. I thought that, if Jake Murdock made enough money while he was on this expedition to buy a herd as big as he wanted, he'd earn every nickel.

But then, I told myself, he'd never get hold of anything like the amount of money he wanted during this campaign. That just goes to prove that logic often has no relationship to how a thing actually works out.

We rode in rain, we slept in mud and pools of water, and we ate raw bacon and hardtack. Some of the infantry fell out of the line of march and lay in the mud without moving. Those boys would have died right where they fell if they hadn't been loaded on pack horses or travois.

Many of the cavalry horses were so played out they were shot and left beside the road to rot. This, of course, put many a cavalrymen on foot so they had to slog along through the mud the same as the infantry.

I kept telling myself that I was better off than the men in uniform. At least I wasn't under the strict discipline they were; I had far more freedom of movement than they did. Still, even for me, it was as near hell as I ever wanted to be.

We had hooked up with Terry's command that included a remnant of the 7th Cavalry under Major Reno. This gave us 4,000 men, but it wouldn't have made any difference if it had been ten times that. Mired down the way we were, or slowed down anyway with sick men and played-out horses, it was ridiculous to think we would ever catch any Indians.

We moved from the Rosebud to the Tongue and on to the Powder where we found grass, and on the afternoon of August 17th we reached the Yellowstone. Later in the day the *Far West* steamed up from the mouth of the Tongue. All of us, scouts and soldiers alike, felt better just to see something that proved the whole world hadn't turned back to wilderness.

It was Crook's idea to follow an Indian trail toward the Little Missouri, so we separated from Terry's command. We packed fifteen days' rations and marched up the Powder, crossed it, then turned east toward the Little Missouri. The Crows and Shoshones left us, figuring that their homes back in the Big Horn country were safe, now that the Sioux had pulled out.

Buffalo Bill left us, too. Several of us scouts gave each other the wink. I guess the correspondents missed him, but we expected him to pull out. Campaigning in the rain and cold and mud was not to his liking. He said he had some theatrical engagements to fill. Maybe so. I'll admit he was a good actor. I told Murdock I thought Cody belonged on the stage and Murdock agreed, then said if he ever showed up in Cheyenne for a theater engagement, he'd go down there and tell them the truth.

I told Murdock he'd better save himself the trouble, that people wanted to be fooled. He admitted I was right about that. Anyhow, Cody got on the steamer and headed down the Yellowstone toward civilization. I never saw him again.

We marched through some of the worst gumbo I ever saw. It stuck to the soldiers' boots and horses' hoofs until it was an effort to take each step. Thunder and lightning, and then all of a sudden a hell of a rainstorm hit us that made me think someone up there had turned on a heavenly faucet.

I rode on ahead with Murdock and Grouard, and much to my surprise we crossed an Indian trail that was considerably fresher than the one we had been following. I suppose the rain and cold had been as hard on the Sioux as it had on us and we had partly closed the gap.

We turned north on Beaver Creek, then east up Andrew's Creek, and on September 4th we reached and crossed the Little Missouri. Still it rained. Our clothes were wearing out. We didn't have anything to wear except what we had on. We'd take our clothes off and wash them when we had a chance, and stand around naked until they dried, if the rain would let up enough for them to dry.

Murdock had picked up a hacking cough that shook his big body and made him sore all over. It seemed to me that almost every man in the command was sick with something, dysentery or rheumatic fever or just a bad cold. I wasn't very anxious to catch up with the Indians because I didn't believe our outfit could put up much of a fight, as sick and tired and worn out as we were.

When we finally turned south toward the Black Hills, we just about forgot we were out here after Indians. All we could think of was getting some place where there was food and shelter and clean clothes.

We had two and one half days' rations, and we were at least seven full days from the Black Hills. We went on half rations, but Crook frankly admitted we'd be eating our horses before we got there.

Sundown had proved himself a tough horse. He had held up well, much better than the average horse in the expedition, and I decided right then that I'd kill the first man who had the notion he'd eat Sundown. I guess everybody understood how I felt because I didn't kill anybody.

Most of the men didn't take the idea of eating horse meat seriously at first, but before long the hardtack was gone. Our bacon had been eaten days ago. The rain continued and the small amount of salt and sugar we still had was washed away. Horse meat was the alternative, so we ate it without salt and we were glad to have it.

We weren't looking for Indians, but we ran into a sizeable bunch at Slim Buttes just the same and wound up in quite a fight, losing about thirty men. The Indians suffered considerably, so I guess we made a good fight of it. The Sioux must have decided it wasn't going to be another Custer affair, so they pulled out and we went on, thinking more about finding something to eat than of smashing the Sioux.

One good result of the battle was the fact that we wound up with some Indian ponies and buffalo robes and even a little food that they left behind them, but nothing really changed. The rain kept right on falling. It was enough to make a man wonder why this country wasn't a swamp instead of being close to a desert as it obviously was. We weren't quite as hungry as we had been, but we were just as cold and wet and miserable as we had been for days.

The first ridges of the Black Hills were visible to the south of us now, but we were still a long way from the closest settlements. I was more concerned than ever about Murdock. His face was flushed, and I was sure he had a fever along with his cough. Murdock had lost a good deal of weight so his skin seemed to be pulled over his big bones. His roan had held up about as well as Sundown, but it was all Murdock could do to stay in the saddle. He swayed back and forth like a sack of wool. I watched him closely because I was afraid he was going to fall off his horse.

For once I thought he had forgotten all about the JM and his big dreams. I guess that was what worried me more than anything else. When he quit thinking about the JM, he was a mighty sick man. I didn't expect him to live long enough to get to Deadwood.

Chapter Thirteen

We camped sixteen miles north of Crook City, the most northern of the mining camps in the Black Hills. General Crook had gone on with his staff and a small escort, having received orders to meet General Sheridan at Fort Laramie as soon as possible. It was plain to me that, if I didn't get Murdock into a bed, he was a dead man, so I asked and received permission to take him to Crook City.

I saddled Sundown and Murdock's roan, then got Murdock into the saddle, although I wasn't sure he'd stay there. The rain had stopped, and that was something for which I was truly thankful. Still, it was a tough night.

We followed a road of sorts through scattered timber. Three times Murdock stopped his horse and got off and lay down. He swore he couldn't go another foot. He coughed and wheezed and fought for breath, and, when he was finally able to talk, he said for me to go on.

I told him I wasn't going to budge without him

and for him to get back on his horse. He did, after a good deal of pushing and heaving on my part. Although he had lost a lot of weight, he was still a heavy man. We'd go a few miles at a slow walk, and then we'd have it to do all over again.

By the time we reached Crook City, the sun was up. It wasn't much of a town, just a bunch of frame houses and log cabins scattered haphazardly in the bottom of a draw. There were some pines growing among the houses and a fair stand of timber on the slopes on both sides of the town. At first I thought the place was deserted, then I decided everybody was still sleeping, although that seemed strange for a mining camp.

I finally found what claimed to be a hotel, an ugly, two-story frame building. An old man with a peg leg was swamping out the bar. He sloshed a bucket of dirty water into the street and headed back inside. I yelled at him. He kept going until I yelled again and told him I'd shoot his good leg off it he didn't stand still and answer a question for me.

He set the bucket down and looked me over. I guess Murdock and I were a tough-looking pair with ragged beards and long hair and dirty clothes that were ready to fall off us. He said: "I dunno if you're part of Crook's expedition or a pair of road agents. You're about as hard-looking as he was last night. His officers, too." He spat into the street in disgust. "I dunno what's happened to the United States Army, but I fought through most of the war. I didn't lose my leg till the Wilderness. I can tell you that I never did see a general look like he looked. Not even U.S. Grant."

I hadn't come to defend General Crook. I said:

"I've got a sick friend who needs a doctor. Where'll I find one?"

He jerked a hand off to the south. "Deadwood. It's sixteen miles from here."

I looked at Murdock. He sat hunched over his saddle horn, coughing and moaning and fighting for breath. His head was tipped forward so his chin was almost on his chest. I figured he was just about ready to fall out of the saddle.

"He'll never make it," I said. "I'd better take a room here in the hotel. Maybe, if I put him in bed for a while, he could stand the trip later in a wagon."

The old man was scratching the back of his neck, looking at me and then at Murdock and back to me. He said: "There's a woman who lives down the street a piece in that white frame house." He jerked a thumb in the general direction. "She ain't no doctor, but she's purty close. She's taken care of some sick men since she got here with her brother last June. Her name's Emily Durling. Mebbe you oughta go see her."

"Thanks," I said. "I will."

We rode down the street, Murdock gripping the horn with his left hand. I doubt that he'd understood anything we'd just said. I had a feeling he was close to being unconscious. His eyes were as expressionless as if they were glass. He labored for every breath so I had a horrible fear each was going to be his last one.

The minute we reined up in front of the white frame house, Murdock's left hand loosened his grip on the horn and he toppled out of the saddle to the ground before I could get to him. He was completely limp when I lifted his head and shoulders off the ground and dragged him toward the house.

Before I reached the front door, it opened and a woman stepped out. She was one of the biggest women I ever saw, six feet tall and heavy-boned. Not fat. Just big. She took one look at us and said: "I'll help you."

She picked up Murdock's feet and we carried him into the house. She jerked her head at the bedroom to my left. "In there."

We laid him on the bed. I asked: "You're Emily Durling?"

"Yes," she answered. "I don't know what you've been told, but I'm not a doctor. I am the nearest thing to it in this sorry collection of people who are trying to scratch a living out of the ground or out of each other."

I took a good look at her then. She was about thirty-five, I judged. Not pretty at all, but not ugly, either. By that I mean her features were regular and she had a good complexion and she didn't have a mustache or a mole or a scar or anything that disfigured her. She was just a big, strong, healthy woman who seemed kindly enough. I guess she stood three or four inches taller than me, and maybe that was the reason the thought struck me that she was a woman a man just wouldn't want to get into bed with.

"We were scouts for the Crook expedition," I said. "I was told there was a doctor in Deadwood, but he'd never get there the shape he's in."

"No, he wouldn't," she agreed.

"I'm Bill Lang," I said. "I'll go get a room in the hotel. His name is Jake Murdock. He's got money . . ."

"I'll do the best I can for him," she broke in tartly, "and you'd better know right now that money is no object."

I turned toward the door and stopped. A man stood there staring at me. Well, he looked like a man. Sort of, anyway. He was little, maybe five feet tall and hunchbacked with a pale face and very sharp black eyes that had a way of boring into me.

"That's right, my friend," he said. "Money is no object to us whatever. We have all there is in the world."

Emily Durling sighed. "This is my brother Lacey, Mister Lang. He lives with me and helps me care for the sick." She motioned to the door. "You run along. Come on, Lacey, and help me get his clothes off."

I went outside, thinking this was a strange pair. I mounted Sundown and, leading the roan, rode back up the street until I found a livery stable. I went through the archway and dismounted as a man walked along the runway toward me, yawning and rubbing is face.

"A double bait of oats," I said. "Rub down both of them good. They'll be here a while, so you take care of them."

"Kind o' skinny, ain't they?" He yawned again. "I didn't sleep much last night. General Crook was here with his staff and some more officers and we . . ."

"Yeah, I know," I said.

I went into the hotel dining room and wolfed down the biggest breakfast I ever had in my life, then I stepped into the bar. Old Peg Leg had finished swamping the place out and was gone, but there was a man behind the bar washing glasses. I ordered a drink. The bartender served me and then started off about last night and the big shindig in honor of General Crook because the town was named after him and he was on his way south.

"I know," I said, and didn't try to sound polite. "Now I want to know something about Emily Durling and her brother Lacey."

He put his cloth down and glared at me, his eyes getting narrow and turning ugly. He said: "I don't know why you want to know anything about Emily Durling or what you want to know, but I figure it ain't none of your business. There ain't a man in this camp who don't worship her, and I ain't standing still for a saddle bum . . ."

"You can hold it right there," I said. "I just had breakfast, so I'm not hungry for the first time in weeks, but I'm tired and sleepy and I'm mean. My friend and I have been chasing Indians with Crook since last May, and now, by God, I don't aim to be called a saddle bum. You'd better answer my question."

The bartender's mouth sprung open as I dropped my hand to the butt of my gun. He swallowed twice, and then he said in a squeaky voice: "I didn't know you were with the general. Well, now, there ain't much to tell about Miss Emily except she never turned nobody away who needed looking after. I guess she was a nurse in the war. Anyhow, she knows a lot about taking care of sick people."

"Married?"

"No. She's an old maid."

"What about her brother?"

"He's like a lot of men who are bunged up one way or another. He's kind of ornery sometimes and he'd like to gamble, only Miss Emily, she don't give him much money. He don't do nothing 'cept chop wood and run errands and such for his sister."

"Are they rich?"

"Rich?" He laughed. "No, I don't figure they are, but Miss Emily does seem to have all the money she needs. She's got one of the best houses in town and she never worries about being paid after taking care of anybody."

I stood there, staring at my drink and trying to make some sense out of it. You just don't expect to find people like Emily and Lacey Durling in a mining camp. Finally I asked: "Why did they come here?"

He looked at me as if he considered that a stupid question, then he shook his head. "Well, now that you ask, I dunno. I never heard Miss Emily say."

I took a room, figuring I'd sleep two, three hours, then go see how Murdock was. If he was better, I'd get a wagon and take him to Deadwood, but I was asleep the minute my head hit the pillow and I didn't wake up until it was dark. I'd slept the clock around. If I hadn't been worried about Murdock, I could have slept it around again I do believe.

Chapter Fourteen

I soon gave up any notion I had about taking Murdock to Deadwood. He was in a delirium most of the time for three days. When he wasn't, he lay on his back, his eyes closed, not moving and not knowing anything.

I was scared. I'd never been around a sick man in my life, so I didn't know what to expect. Of course, it was worse with Jake Murdock than it would have been with most men because normally he was a giant of a man who didn't depend on anybody to do anything for him.

Emily wasn't worried. "There isn't much we can do," she said. "I've put some cold cloths on his forehead, hoping it would bring his fever down. They did cool him off some. I've got a mustard plaster on his chest, but mostly it's a matter of him resting and letting his body have a chance to heal."

She was quite a woman, this Emily Durling. I took to her right away. Not that I understood her. She was a puzzle to me and to the whole camp as near as I could tell. I called her Emily the second day and she called me Bill, and it seemed we were good friends from the beginning.

We'd sit beside Murdock's bed while I smoked and she knitted and he groaned and rolled around. We'd talk a little but most of the time we wouldn't say a word for maybe an hour, and either way I felt good just sitting there with Emily doing nothing. It was a rare feeling for me, especially with a woman.

I got a bath and a shave and a haircut the next morning, and I bought new clothes and burned my old ones. I bought new duds for Murdock and took them to the Durling house. Emily said: "You look like another man. I don't believe you're an outlaw, after all."

I laughed. I guess that was about what everybody thought of us, even of General Crook and his staff. It was hard for anyone to realize what we'd been through, and, when I told Emily, she said: "I don't see how you got through as well as you did. It's a miracle you're not as sick as your friend."

"I was cold and hungry and tired," I said, "and I had a sore throat. One night I was wet and I began to shiver and I couldn't stop, but the next day I felt better. Jake just kept getting a little worse."

"He'll be all right," she said, "but if you hadn't got him here when you did, he wouldn't have made it."

"Funny how a big man like him would get sicker than me," I said. "When he's well, he's the strongest man I ever ran into. He could break me in two."

She smiled. "You're tough and he isn't as far as disease is concerned. The fact that a man is big and strong under normal conditions has nothing to do with how easily he'll come down with something."

I stayed in Crook City for a week. I spent most of the time in Murdock's room sitting in a rocking chair, and most of that time Emily was beside me in another chair. After he came to himself, Murdock couldn't remember much about the last week of the campaign and he remembered nothing at all of our night ride to Crook City.

I told him what had happened and that General Crook had gone to Fort Laramie and the column had moved through Crook City and gone on south. It was commanded now by General Merritt. I didn't know where they were headed, but I supposed it was Camp Robinson.

He was soon eating everything Emily would give him and usually he was hollering for more. She wouldn't let him have anything but chicken broth and such at first, but later she allowed him solid food and he began regaining his strength. Emily wouldn't even guess when he could make the ride home. I was getting more and more certain that I'd have to go on and he could come later in the fall when he felt like it.

I didn't mention it, though. As a matter of fact, I enjoyed the rest and I discovered that the long campaign and the constant exposure to rain and cold and lack of decent food had taken more out of me than I realized. Murdock often dozed in bed, and, now that I knew Emily a little better, we'd talk a blue streak until it was time for me to go back to the hotel.

She told me about her nursing experience during the war and how she wanted to be a doctor, but it was a world made for men. The fact that she was big and strong as most men had nothing to do with the situation. She had found the doors closed as far as being trained as a doctor was concerned. The more I talked to her and watched her with Murdock, the more I realized that she could come nearer healing a sick man than most doctors could.

She admitted that she could and actually bragged about it. She said: "I realized that there is much to be discovered about healing, but I also know that most doctors don't use even some simple facts that I have discovered about curing the sick. I'm sure these facts are not secrets."

"For instance?" I asked.

"For one thing, rest is of major importance in a case like this," she answered. "Having a great faith that a sick person is going to get well is a factor." Then she looked at me and added: "Don't laugh, but so is prayer. What any doctor should realize, and most of them don't, is that a human being is not just a physical body. We have to treat the sick from the standpoint of the patient's having a mind and a spirit as well as a body. In other words, the whole person, not just the flesh and blood and bone that make up the physical body." She laid her knitting in her lap and leaned forward to stare at me. She said: "I have seen a few doctors who might be called inspired. I mean, they seemed to do the right thing by intuition, but most doctors only know how to cut a person open and operate. If they can't do that, they dose him with calomel and leave him. If the patient recovers, it's God's doing, not the doctor's."

When I first saw Emily, I thought she was just another big, strong woman, neither beautiful nor ugly, but now I looked at her, and so help me she was beautiful. I don't know how or why, but it was a kind of radiance that possessed her and made a bright shine. I wasn't sure whether she or I was crazy. All I knew was that I had a strange feeling about her that I had never had before.

The truth was I didn't have the slightest idea what she was talking about. What I knew about God and prayer and faith you could stick in your eye. As far as I was concerned, a human being was a body. I'd shot some bodies full of holes and I'd seen the men die. I'd had a hole shot in my body and I'd been mighty slow getting over it. I had seen plenty of men and some Indian women and children shot full of holes on this expedition. I hadn't seen any minds or spirits that Emily was talking about, although the Sioux seemed to know more about spirits than we did.

I knocked my pipe out, then I said: "Why don't you tell doctors what you know?"

She laughed and sat back in her chair and went on knitting. After a while she said: "And be crucified because I'm ahead of my time? No thank you. I'll go on the way I am and do as much good as I can."

Before the week was out, I discovered she was a strange mixture. She was very impatient with her brother. I'll admit Lacey was a mess. He took advantage of his hunchback to play on people's sympathy and he wouldn't do a stroke of work if he could figure a way to get out of it.

Sometimes Lacey was downright ornery. He was sassy, and, if Emily didn't have a meal on time, he'd insult her. One night he came home drunk. Emily didn't say a word. She doused him with cold water, yanked off his clothes, and threw him into bed. She jerked the covers over him and stalked out of his room, slamming the door behind her.

"If I find out who sold him that whiskey, I'll kill the bastard," she said.

I was shocked. It was the only time in the week I spent in Crook City that I knew her to lose her temper, and it was the only time I ever heard her use the word bastard. If she had known right then who had sold Lacey the whiskey, she might have killed him. She would at least have beaten him half to death.

The next morning she apologized and said: "Every bartender in this camp knows that Lacey is not to have a drink and he is not to gamble, but they don't always do what they're supposed to." She shook her head and added sadly: "It's a poor camp, Bill. Not much money being made. A lot of houses are empty. The gulch has been worked out, and, unless they figure a way to get water from Spearfish Creek into Whitewood Creek, Crook City is a dead camp."

"How did you happen to come out here to the Black Hills in the first place?" I asked.

She fidgeted around for a few seconds, then she said: "I thought there wouldn't be a doctor in a small camp like this, so I might be of some use. You know, if you're not of some use, you might just as well be dead. That's the way with Lacey. He feels so sorry for himself he won't do anything, so he isn't any good to himself or anybody else." She walked to the stove and poured a cup of coffee and handed it to me. She said: "Our mother took care of Lacey until she died last winter. Now I have to look after him. It's not easy. I know he has a lot of aches and pains and he's not strong and he doesn't look like much, but he doesn't have to keep on being so sorry for himself. He could live a worthwhile life if he wanted to. We have some money, quite a bit of money in fact. It came to us when Mamma died. She left it in my name and Lacey has to depend on me for every cent he gets and that makes him hate me."

For a minute she stood at the stove rubbing her chin; then she turned and gave me just a hint of a grin. "And I guess I came here partly to find a husband, but the men in this camp are a sorry lot, digging all day in the ground for a few dollars in gold. A very sorry lot."

She was right about that. I hadn't been around mining camps much, but it did seem to me that the men I had seen in the hotel and the saloons were living from hand to mouth, both the businessmen and the miners. I wondered what would happen to them when winter came.

I could understand how she wouldn't be likely to find a man here who would attract her, but I could also understand how it was that most men would shy away from her. I liked her, but I wouldn't marry her, so I guess I ended up feeling sorry for her.

By the end of the week Murdock had regained some of his strength and a few of the pounds he'd lost. Emily had cut his hair and trimmed his beard, so he looked a little more like himself. He could walk as far as the front room and sit in a rocking chair beside a window for an hour before he began to get dizzy and had to be helped back to bed.

The last night I was there, he said: "Bill, every day I figure I'll be as skookum as I used to be but, damn it, seems like the progress I make is mighty slow. It'll be three weeks, maybe a month, before I've got enough steam to stay on a horse long enough to ride to the JM."

I nodded. I'd been thinking I'd better go on. No use of me staying there because I couldn't do anything for him, and he was out of danger now. He just needed time and a lot of Emily's good cooking. He hadn't said a word about Ellie or the JM or Charley Three Horses. As far as I knew, he hadn't even written to Ellie since he'd left the JM last May. I was concerned about her if he wasn't.

"Emily's taking good care of you," I said. "I might as well ride out in the morning."

"Yeah, you might as well," he agreed in an absentminded tone as if he had his mind on something else.

I guess he did, although at the time I didn't know what it was. In the morning I paid my hotel and livery stable bills and rode south. My Indian-chasing days were behind me. I was glad of that. They were days I didn't care to live over or even think about.

Chapter Fifteen

The week of rest and having all the oats he could eat put a lot of vinegar into Sundown. He was glad to leave the livery stable and get on the road again, so we hit a good pace and held it all the way to Deadwood. It was a good-size town, larger than I had expected to see. I was told there were 2,000 people in and around Deadwood, and I guessed that many or more.

The town was a rough one as many new mining camps are. It had one long street with frame houses and log cabins on both sides. There was a big business district for a town of its size with the usual number of hell holes that would and could relieve a miner of his dust in short order. The street lay in the bottom of a ravine with timbered hills on both sides. I had the feeling that, if Deadwood grew, it would be on the ends of the street, but not on the sides.

I tarried long enough to buy supplies that I tied behind my saddle and rode on. The scenery was beautiful, but I wasn't of a mind to enjoy it, so I camped only when necessary, ate when I was hungry, let Sundown graze when I figured he had to, and put the miles behind me as fast as I could. Then I was out of the foothills. I forded South Cheyenne River and headed straight south for Camp Robinson.

I laid over a day, even though the closer I got to the Chug, the more anxious I was to see Ellie. I'm not sure why I felt the way I did, but the word *home* kept popping up in my mind. Now I didn't have the slightest reason to call the JM home. It didn't belong to me. Maybe half of it would, if Murdock talked me into the partnership deal he had offered, but I had made up my mind I wouldn't have any part of it.

Murdock was the kind of man who would call the shots in a partnership, especially since the JM was his to begin with. He could say, and with some logic, that he was the senior member of the firm regardless of how much money I put into the deal.

I had no intention of investing my money—and I had a little over $2,500 in my money belt—in a cattle ranch and then playing second fiddle the rest of my life. I had also made up my mind I was not going back to hiring my gun out to any land-hogging cowman the way I had on the Picketwire. Beyond that I hadn't decided about my future.

They told me at Camp Robinson that it wasn't safe to travel alone, and maybe it wasn't. Certainly there was a chance some of the young, outlaw Indians located at the Red Cloud Agency would sneak off the reservation and raise hell, and it was also possible that small bands of hostile Sioux might not have gone on north toward Canada and were hiding in the Black Hills or the broken country between the

Hills and the Powder River. A greater danger and a very real one was from the road agents.

Foolish or not, I did ride alone to Fort Laramie and from there to the Chug.

I rode into the JM yard in the middle of an afternoon in late September. I saw smoke rising from the chimney an inch or two before it was swept away by the wind, so Ellie was there just as I had been sure she would be. I rode on past the house to the barn and dismounted. Charley Three Horses heard me and stepped outside. When he saw who it was, he held out his hand.

"Welcome," Charley said, and for one of the few times in his life a broad grin brightened his dark face.

"I'm glad to get here," I said, being careful to avoid using the word home.

He looked at me and then back along the road, and asked: "Murdock?"

"He won't be here for a while," I said. "It'll be three, four weeks. He got sick right at the end of the campaign and he couldn't come yet, but he'll be along. He's all right."

Charley nodded and took the reins. "Good horse?" he asked.

I patted Sundown on the neck. I said: "Charley, you'll never know how good a horse he is. He saved my life during the campaign. A lot of horses just quit. We killed some and ate them. We'd have starved to death if we hadn't, but Sundown held up the best of any of them."

He nodded again as if that was what he had expected. "You stay?" he asked.

"I'll stay till Murdock gets back," I said, not

knowing what else to say because I wasn't sure what I was going to do.

"You take care of things," he said. "Charley's pulling out." He motioned toward the Laramie range. "I got a horse ranch."

I didn't know what he was talking about, but I didn't care, so I didn't ask. I said: "Sure, I'll take care of things."

I wheeled and ran to the house. Ellie may have been cooking or just daydreaming. Anyhow, she hadn't looked out of the window and hadn't seen or heard me until I opened the door and went in and closed it behind me. She was standing beside the stove with her back to me until she heard the door, then she whirled around.

For an instant she stood there staring at me and I stood looking at her. She was just as pretty as when I'd left the JM and I told myself as I had many times during the summer that Jake Murdock couldn't be stupid enough to send her to the reservation. But I knew he was.

"Bill!" she screamed as soon as she got over the shock of seeing me.

I opened my arms to her and she ran to me and fell against me. I hugged her and then I kissed her and she kissed me back, and I lost track of time. All I knew was that I'd been right. This was home for me and this was why I had hurried back and why I hadn't allowed myself to be slowed up by traveling with someone else after leaving Camp Robinson. It was worth all the risk I had taken.

After a while she pulled away from me and wiped her eyes and said: "It's been such a long time. Bill, I didn't think you and Jake would ever come back. I was afraid you were dead." She swallowed and wiped her eyes again, and asked in a whisper: "Where is Jake?"

I told her and it took quite a bit of talking to convince her that he was all right and he'd be along when he was strong enough to ride. She kept shaking her head and saying: "Jake has never been sick. Not since I came here."

I'd go over it again. About having almost nothing to eat and being wet day after day and not getting any sleep, and how his cough had racked his body until he'd been sore all over. Then she asked: "What about this woman where he's living? This Emily Durling?"

"She's a nurse." I'd told her that before, but I told her again. "She's as big as a horse, but she's a good woman. She's taking good care of him."

"I'll bet she is," Ellie said, her lips curling. "I'll bet she is."

Charley Three Horses came in then and walked across the room to the shelves of food beside the stove. He began to help himself, pretty liberally, I thought. Ellie went to him and talked a while.

I couldn't hear what they were saying, but after he threw some grub into a sack, he wheeled and walked out of the room. Ellie had done all the talking. I don't think Charley had said a word. I watched him from a window. He had a fine black gelding in front, saddled up and ready to ride. He tied the sack of grub behind the saddle and mounted and rode off.

"He worked hard all summer," Ellie said. "I guess he thought Jake would send his pay home with you. Anyhow, he's found a little valley with grass and good water back in the hills and he says he'll have a horse ranch. He's got his brand on a few now." She looked straight at me then, and asked: "Do you think they'll let a 'breed have a horse ranch?"

"I don't know," I said.

I didn't, either. I knew how most of the people in this country felt about the half-breeds and I figured they wouldn't get a fair deal any way you looked at it, but the horse ranch was Charley's business. It sure wasn't mine to give him any advice unless he asked for it, and he hadn't. What was more, he wouldn't.

Ellie shrugged. "Well, Charley will do what he wants to and I can't stop him." Suddenly she seemed to be conscience-stricken, and said: "Bill, I'll bet you're hungry. Why didn't you ask me to feed you?"

"I'll wait till you're ready to eat," I said.

She laughed softly and came to me again and put her hands on my shoulders. She said: "Bill, you almost died when you came here last spring. I thought for a while you were going to, but I took care of you and I saved you. Now you belong to me."

I took her into my arms again. "Sure, Ellie," I said. "I belong to you."

I kissed her again and I knew I could have her. I knew it just as certainly as I had known it last spring when I sat beside her and Murdock was gone, and it came to me that all I had to do was to ask and she'd go to the bunk with me. But it had been different then. Now I knew what Murdock was figuring to do and I knew what I was going to do, and that threw a different light on the whole business.

I took her hand and led her toward the bunk. My belly was empty, but my hunger for food was not as great as the other hunger that possessed me.

Chapter Sixteen

For several days I cut wood and pumped water and fed and watered the stock. Charley Three Horses had the chores well in hand so there wasn't much for me to do and I began to fret about the future.

Winter was coming on and I wasn't sure what I'd be doing when the bad weather hit. I did know one thing. I was not staying on the JM until spring. I could go to Fort Laramie and hire a man to stay here till Murdock got back. The problem was I didn't know when that would be. I couldn't go off and leave Ellie here with a stranger.

I wooled it around in my head every day. Finally I did know what I had to do. After dinner one day I said: "Ellie, marry me. Go away with me. I'll find someone to look after things here until Jake gets back."

She stared at me as if I had said something or done something that was evil. She said: "Bill, you know I can't marry you. Jake will marry me someday. I won't sleep with you any more when I'm married to Jake, but I thought it was all right to do it now."

I assured her that it was. I leaned back in my chair and filled my pipe and wondered how in hell I was going to tell her what she had to know. She'd probably think I was lying, just telling her so she would marry me, but I knew I had to try.

"You told me I belonged to you," I said finally. "I do. I love you, Ellie. I want to marry you and take care of you." I paused long enough to strike a match and light my pipe, and then added: "And I want a family."

She looked at me hard then, maybe not quite sure if I meant it. I don't think Murdock had ever told her he loved her or ever said he wanted to take care of her, and I'm sure he never told her he wanted a family. In a way she was a lost soul. I doubt that she expected any white man to say that to her, and of course she would never look at a half-breed or an Indian.

"Thank you, Bill," she said in a low tone. "You do belong to me, but I'll have to give you to some other woman. You've forgotten that I belong to Jake."

I let her have it then, right between the eyes. It was a cruel thing to do, but it had to be done sometime, and I didn't see any sense in putting if off.

"Listen to me, Ellie," I said. "You don't belong to Jake. He doesn't want you any more. Times are changing. You've told me that. Jake wants a white wife. He's going to send you to the reservation."

She shrank back as if I had struck her. She whispered: "No, he'll never do that. Other ranchers around here have, but Jake won't."

"He promised to marry you," I said. "He hasn't and he won't. You really know that, don't you?"

She nodded and bowed her head. "I guess I do," she said, "but I'll go on living with him whether he marries me or not. I'll never leave him. Don't you see how it is, Bill? He gave me a home when I needed one. He's always treated me good. He's never beaten me the way most of the white men have beaten their squaws."

"You don't owe him a damned thing," I said angrily, "and quit thinking of yourself as a squaw. You've worked hard for him and he was satisfied with you as long as everything went the way it always has, but by next summer the herds will be coming in, there'll be big spreads all the way from Cheyenne north to Montana, and Jake won't let you stay here. He's ambitious. You know that. Someday he may be governor. Or senator or congressman. You think he can run for office while he's living with a part-Indian woman?"

She began to cry. She got up and walked to the stove and stood with her back to me. I wasn't proud of myself. I'd hurt her and I was sorry, but I knew Jake Murdock was going to hurt her far worse than I had. I put my pipe down and went to her and took her into my arms.

"Honey," I said, "I didn't say anything to you last spring. When I began getting over my wound, I wanted you so bad it hurt, but I didn't know how things were going to shape up. I do now. Jake hasn't said so in plain words, but I know what he's going to do. That's why I asked you to marry me."

Still she stood there as stiff as a poker in my arms.

The tears were running down her cheeks and once in a while a sob would shake her rigid body. Then I said: "Ellie, I've never thought of you as a squaw. You're a good, capable woman. A pretty one, too. Any man should be proud to have you as his wife, but as far as we're concerned the important thing is I love you."

She whirled and buried her face in my shirt and cried. When she could talk, she wiped her eyes and stepped back from me. She said: "I'll always remember what you've said. I love you, but I love Jake, too. No matter how he treats me or what he says or does, I can't marry you."

"Not if he sends you back to the reservation?"

"He won't."

"But if he does?"

"He can't make me go. I won't go. "I'll . . . I'll kill myself first."

"Ellie, promise me this. If it does happen, let me take care of you."

"I'll promise that," she said as if she were sure it was a promise she wouldn't have to keep.

"Don't forget it," I said. "I'm going over to Rand's place. I'll be back for supper."

I don't know why I went to Rand's ranch except that I had to do something, go somewhere, and I couldn't go as far as Cheyenne or Fort Laramie. Besides, I thought that Ellie would want to be alone for a while, and of course I couldn't leave her overnight.

Rand had the biggest ranch on the Chug. He had been here longer than Murdock and he'd started with a fair-size herd of cattle and a Sioux woman. He'd got rid of his squaw last spring and he'd sold most of his cattle to the Army. Now he lived alone in a big, two-story house made of grout, a kind of local cement. He had a sprawling barn and a maze of corrals and some fine meadow land along the Chug, but now he didn't have much of a herd.

He was in the barn working on some harness when he saw me ride up. He dropped the copper rivets and his hammer and came out to meet me as I dismounted. We'd talked a couple of times before when I'd been there with Murdock last May, but I didn't know him very well.

He was a fat cowboy, something you seldom see, and I doubt that he was particularly ambitious. Or maybe he was disillusioned as a cowman. You can make it big in the cattle business, or you can work your tail off just to keep afloat, and that was the position Rand had been in.

He had built well, as if he had planned to make something out of the place and wanted to live here forever, but now it had a run-down look about it, and I had a hunch he was happy to have the cash and fewer cattle as a result of his sale to the Army in the spring. I thought that if he had half the drive that Murdock had, everything around here would have looked differently.

We shook hands and he asked: "Where's Murdock?"

I told him about the campaign, and Murdock's being sick, and then I said: "When I was at Camp Robinson, they were talking about a winter campaign. That's the only way the Sioux can be beaten. You burn their lodges and the grub they've collected and maybe, if you're lucky, you capture their pony herd, and, after they're cold enough and hungry enough, they'll go back to the reservation."

He nodded agreement and dug his pipe out of his pocket and filled it. He said: "Let's go into the house. I've got some coffee left from breakfast."

I shook my head. "Thanks, but I've got to get back. I was wondering what you think will happen next year. By spring the Indian danger will be a thing of the past. Jake keeps saying the big herds will come in then and take over the country. What do you think?"

"Sure they will, but that ain't all that's gonna happen," he said. "Well, maybe not next summer, but in the next three, four years the farmers will come, too. There'll be an irrigation system to put water on the flat west of the JM. That's good land and it can be put under a ditch without any big engineering problems. We'll need a reservoir and we'll fill it from the Laramie. We'll advertise and people will flock in here. Good, solid people. Families, I'm talking about. That means a town and a town means business."

I could see he wasn't hoorawing me any. I guess he wasn't a cowman at heart the way Murdock was, and he aimed to get in on the ground floor when this development came. I said: "It'll take money."

"Sure." He nodded. "But there's always money whenever you can promise a reasonable profit. Now you take this Slim Galt. He's staked out Galt City and he's . . ."

"I never heard of it," I said. "Or him, either."

"He came in last summer," Rand said, "not long after you and Jake left. Right now he ain't got nothing but his store and two, three shacks he's put up, but he'll have a town there. Fact is, I've bought three lots across the street from his store and I'm gonna

put me up a saloon as soon as I can sell out here."
He screwed up his mouth and squinted at me, then
he said: "You wouldn't know it, but that bastard's
got money. When the time's right, he'll put in the
reservoir and the ditch system. You'd be smart to in-
vest in a few of his lots yourself, Lang."

I thought about it all the way back to the JM. I
thought about it hard. As far as money was concerned, it had always been easy come, easy go with
me, but it was different now. It hadn't been easy,
making those rides from Crook's camp to Fort Fetterman and back, and the *dinero* that was in my
money belt wasn't multiplying very fast.

I had heard about men investing in town lots and
becoming rich, and I started thinking it might just
as well be my destiny to be rich as to be poor. I knew
the land on that flat was good land and would raise
wheat and other crops. The development would
have to wait on a railroad, but sooner or later a railroad would be built north of Cheyenne into
Wyoming.

By the time I got back to the JM, I decided I'd go
take a look at Galt City. I had a hunch that Carl Rand
knew what he was talking about.

Chapter Seventeen

As soon as we finished breakfast in the morning, I said: "I'm going to saddle up and ride over to Galt City. Rand was telling me yesterday that a fellow named Slim Galt has staked out a town site."

She nodded. "He has a store. I've been over there several times with Charley this summer to buy supplies. Harness up the team and take the buckboard. I'll go with you. I'm out of some things."

I did. The day was a pleasant one with a blue sky and no wind. It was almost hot for October and I thought Ellie deserved to get out of the house. I had ridden across the flat Rand had mentioned a dozen times last spring with Murdock, but I'd never looked at it with the idea that it could be irrigated. Now I did, and, although I was no part of an engineer, I decided Rand was right.

The flat lay on a bench above the Chug. I don't know how big it was, 10,000 acres perhaps, or maybe 12,000, but the main thing that struck me was the obvious fact that a reservoir somewhere to the west at the base of the foothills would be high enough for the water to flow across the flat. As Rand had said, there would be no big engineering problems.

Murdock would probably raise hell because he had figured on this flat being part of his range, but there was plenty of other range he could claim and he sure couldn't hold this if someone laid out a ditch system and farmers moved in and settled on the land.

By the time I got to Galt City, I'd made up my mind that I'd go along on this deal. Sure it was a gamble, but I didn't know of anything you could do to get ahead that wasn't a gamble. I remembered Murdock saying he wouldn't gamble with cards, but he would gamble on the weather and the price of beef.

I was gambling on whether a man like Slim Galt could make a go of a big deal like this. I was gambling on what the railroad did because, if one was built north of Cheyenne and by-passed Galt City and built its own town, we were licked before we started. I was gambling on economic conditions, too. Another panic like the one in 1873 would ruin a development like this.

Galt City was about what I expected. There was one large building, a two-story, frame structure painted white that was the store with living quarters for Galt and his family upstairs. Back of it was a privy, a woodshed, and a good-size barn and corral.

Main Street had been graded some. That is, the sage and grass had been cleared and dust was hock-deep on the horses. Two other streets had been staked out, Grant Street on the north of Main Street and Lincoln Street on the south. Signs and stakes in their proper places identified them or I wouldn't have known they were streets.

Lincoln Street had three houses, or shacks as Rand had called them, one-room frame buildings with privies and woodsheds. Actually they were more than shacks. They were a fair size and painted white with red trim, so after curtains were hung and something was done with their front yards, they wouldn't look so bad. I also noticed that Galt had a well back of the store, probably the only water in town.

"Quite a city," I said as I pulled up in front of the store.

Ellie laughed. "Quite a city, but I think Slim Galt is right. He'll have a town. Or one somewhere in the neighborhood anyway. We never think of many people living around here, but I've seen a dozen rigs tied at the hitch racks on a Saturday afternoon."

That surprised me. It was like Ellie said. I had ridden all over the country with Murdock last spring and I didn't think there were a dozen ranches between Fort Laramie and Cheyenne, but I suppose people lived in some of the draws, and a man wouldn't see them unless he stumbled onto their houses.

I stepped down and tied, noticing that Galt had placed one long hitch pole in front of the store and another one directly across the street, probably in front of the lots Rand owned. He had about fifty feet of boardwalk built in front of the store, but that was all.

We went in. Ellie said: "You go talk to Slim. I'll look over here on the woman's side of the store."

A man came out of the back when he saw us, hesitated as he saw Ellie turn toward the dry goods counter, then he came to me and held out his hand. He said, grinning: "I'm Slim Galt, mayor of Galt City."

I grinned, too. I couldn't help it. He was about the tallest, skinniest, homeliest, most gangling man I had ever seen in my life. He was thirty-five or so, bald across the front of his head with a shock of light brown hair on the back half. He was the least-likely-looking town promoter I could imagine.

His saber-sharp nose made him look almost comical, but he had a human warmth about him that made me like him at once. I've sensed this in only a few men, but you never mistake it. When you do find it, it's always a quality that inspires trust, and makes you overlook the fact that here's a homely man who's a promoter and maybe trying to fast talk you out of every nickel you have.

"Elected unanimously," I said.

He gave my hand a good grip, his gaze running all the way down to my dusty boots and back to my battered old hat that had gone through the campaign with me, then he winked at me and slapped his thigh and guffawed. He said: "Correct. The vote was one to nothing."

"I'm Bill Lang," I said. "I'm staying at the JM. Jake Murdock is still in the Black Hills. He won't be home for another week or two."

He backed off and squinted at me, his gray eyes trying to read my intentions, then he called: "Miss Ellie, I'll get the missus to wait on you."

"No hurry," Ellie said. "I just like to look."

"She'll want to pass the time of day with you anyway," he said, and jerked his head for me to follow him.

I went to the back of the store with him. He motioned to an upended nail keg beside his desk. I sat down on it and he turned to the foot of the stairs and bawled: "Mirandy, Ellie's here!"

"Coming!" a woman bawled back.

The stairs began to tremble as a big woman came down them. She wasn't big the way Emily Durling was big. She was fat. She simply overflowed in all directions. When she saw me, she gave me a friendly smile, and I realized she had a pretty face. She just needed to lose about one hundred pounds.

"This is Bill Lang," Galt said. "My wife Mirandy."

I nodded as I took off my hat and said: "Pleased to meet you, Missus Galt."

"I'm pleased to meet you, Mister Lang," she said. "You're the gunfighter who went off with Jake Murdock to fight the Sioux, ain't you?"

I nodded. "Only I'm not a gunfighter any more, Missus Galt. I decided that's no life for a man who wants a future."

"I'm glad to hear that." She glanced at Ellie, and then asked in a low tone: "What will Jake Murdock do when he gets here? I mean, about us? About Galt City?"

"I couldn't say," I told her. "He won't like it because he figures this flat is part of his range, but I don't know how he can hold it."

"Go on," Galt said to his wife. "Go wait on Ellie."

She hesitated, still studying me as if trying to see clear down into the bottom of my head, but finally she turned and waddled across the store and started talking to Ellie. Galt said: "She's a worrier. This is our second venture. We lost out in New Mexico when we started a town because of the big cattle out-fits. That's why we came here to try again. We're ahead of the big outfits."

"They're coming," I said.

"I don't want to stop them," he said quickly. "All I want is to be let alone to develop my town and an ir-rigation project. So far all the ranchers have told us they're in favor of what I'm doing, that they want a town here so they won't have to go to Cheyenne to buy supplies. The only thing is they have warned me about Murdock, claiming he's a pusher. None of them knows much about you, but they all agreed you have been a gunfighter and I guess that makes them afraid of you." He hesitated, then he added: "Actually there's no reason under the sun why the town and the farmers living on a chunk of irrigated land should conflict with the cattlemen."

I shrugged. Hell, I wasn't interested in the other ranchers or their fears or whether they had any con-flicts with the new town and the farmers. All of that was behind me.

"I want to buy some lots," I said.

"Well, by God."

He sat down at his desk, or rather he kind of fell into his chair and it rolled back against the wall. I thought he was going to faint. He pulled a ban-danna out of his pants pocket and wiped his sweaty face. He looked across the room at his wife and for about a minute he couldn't say a word. I had never seen complete relief come to a man and relax him the way it did Slim Galt.

"You know," he said finally, "I figured you had

come here with a message from Murdock to get off the flat."

"Not me," I said. "Murdock can deliver his own messages. I'm not rich, but this town might grow, and it might make me rich. Rand said you had money and you'd put in a reservoir and a ditch system. I guess farmers will come if they know you can deliver the water, and, if the farmers come, the businessmen will come and the town will grow."

"That's right," he said, "only I don't have the money. I know where I can get it, but it's not quite the same. I propose to start work next spring on the project."

"What about the railroad?" I asked.

"It's coming," he said. "I can't promise the week and day when a locomotive will puff into Galt City, but it's coming. That's the reason I went ahead with this project. I know you're not going to get anywhere with a town site in a farming area unless you've got a railroad."

"I've got one question to ask you," I said, and looked straight at him. "What do you think of 'breeds?"

He was startled. "Well, it depends. If you're asking about Ellie, I'll say we think a lot of her, but if you're asking about Charley Three Horses . . ." He paused, then he said: "I don't know for sure, but he does make me a little uneasy. I guess he's just too much of an Indian."

That satisfied me. It was enough that he judged them as individuals, not just as half-breeds. At least he didn't have the prejudice that most of the people who lived here had.

We talked for half an hour. I wound up buying five

business lots on Main Street and six residential lots on Lincoln Street, one of them holding a house. On the way home Ellie quizzed me about why I wanted the house, but I wouldn't tell her. Not then. I'd tell her when the time came, but this wasn't the time.

Chapter Eighteen

We had just finished eating breakfast on a cold, windy morning in late October when I looked outside and saw Carl Rand riding into the yard. I had noticed a few minutes before that some snowflakes were in the air, and now there were so many that the visibility was cut down until I couldn't see more than twenty yards away.

I didn't have any difficulty recognizing Carl Rand, though. He always rode like a sack of wool. I had a hunch he'd be more at home in the saloon he was figuring on building in Galt City than he would on his ranch.

I got up and put on my hat and sheepskin and went outside. Rand reined up beside me. He said: "Jake's over at my place. He wants you to saddle up and ride over there, *pronto.*"

It made me sore. Murdock was talking like the big cowman he was going to be. He wasn't there yet and it might take him ten years to get there, so I figured he could do the riding in a snowstorm like this as well as I could. Besides, he owed it to Ellie to come here.

"You tell him to go to hell," I said. "He can ride this direction just as easily as I can ride in that direction."

"He can, I reckon," Rand agreed. "It sure ain't no skin off my nose either way, but he rode hard getting here and he's about all in. You'll find him sitting by the fire in my kitchen. He ain't got his strength back from the sickness you said he had." Rand hesitated, glancing at the house and then at me, and finally he leaned down and said: "He bought my ranch. I'm headed for Galt City. I'm gonna build my saloon this fall if I can get the lumber hauled from Cheyenne and the weather ain't too bad to work outside."

That knocked the wind out of me. I couldn't say a word. I just stood there, staring up at Rand, snow hitting me in the face. One thought lodged in my mind and refused to budge: *Buying the Rand Ranch doesn't make any sense. Murdock was going to use his money to buy a bigger herd.*

I guess Rand took my shock for stubbornness. He said: "Lang, you'd better go see Jake. It'll be better for both you and Ellie."

Then he rode off toward Galt City. I went to the barn and saddled Sundown, and all the time I was wondering why Murdock had bought the Rand place, and then I wondered why he hadn't come here. This was his home. His things were here, including the money he had buried. But what bothered me the most was the simple fact that Ellie would be hurt and angry because he hadn't come here to see her the first thing.

The ride to the Rand place was a cold one. A wind had come up and the snow seemed to be running parallel to the surface of the earth and was headed for somewhere in the Nebraska Panhandle. Still, by the time I reined up and tied in front of the Rand house, there was at least an inch on the ground.

I walked around the house to the back door and knocked. Murdock opened the door and said: "Come in, Bill. Come in. Colder'n hell this morning, ain't it? I'm glad I kept pushing last night and rode on in."

He held out his hand and I shook it as I looked him over. He'd shaved off his beard, but his sweeping, reddish brown mustache was the same as always. He was thinner than normal, but he did look a lot better than when I'd left Crook City.

"You're still a mite skinny, looks like," I said.

"That's not all," he admitted. "I still ain't as skookum as I used to be." He motioned to some pegs in the wall. "Hang up your coat and hat and come over here by the stove. There's still a little of Carl's coffee in the pot."

I hung up my hat and coat and walked to the stove. He handed me a steaming cup of coffee, giving me a sidelong glance out of the corner of his eye, then he said: "Well Bill, you're looking well cared for. I guess you got over the campaign all right."

"Yeah, I feel fine," I said, and waited, holding the cup of coffee in my hand.

Murdock leaned back in his chair and filled his pipe, then turned his head to look out of the window. "I guess we're in for it," he said. "By morning we'll have a foot of snow on the ground."

"Looks like it," I said.

He cleared his throat and struck a match and fired his pipe. He puffed a while, giving me that sidelong glance again, and said: "Maybe Carl told you I've bought him out." I nodded, and he went on: "I guess that kind o' surprised you. Well, it surprised me, too. Fact is, I didn't know he wanted to sell and I didn't know about this fly-by-night promoter named Galt coming in. Carl wants to build a saloon and maybe that'll be a good thing for him. He ain't no cowman and that's a fact."

I drank the coffee and set the cup down on top of the warming oven. Something was working down in the bottom of my stomach. I knew I wouldn't like what I was going to hear. Murdock was having too hard a time getting to the point.

He cleared his throat. "I've bought his quarter-section and the cows he's got left which ain't many on account of he purty well cleaned house last spring when the Army was buying beef, but the real reason I bought the outfit was that I wanted the buildings. The headquarters of the JM is gonna be right here. I've got everything I need except a bunk-house and I'll build that sometime this winter. I figure to keep a crew of six to eight men. I won't go after my herd till the grass is up in the spring, but I'll be looking around, and by April I'll know what I'm getting. Maybe I'll even have the herd here by then."

I had started to reach for my pipe, then I dropped my hand. For a minute I wondered if Murdock was drunk. I'd heard him dream his big dreams and I knew better than anybody except maybe Ellie how his mind worked. I had never in all my life known a man who was driven by ambition the way Jake Murdock was, but to talk this way, as if all he had to do was just go out and buy the herd and hire his crew—well, he wasn't drunk. That was the only thing I was sure of.

"Of course, one of the main reasons I bought Carl out was on account of this house," Murdock went on in a kind of offhand tone. "After all, a man can't expect his wife to move into the kind of place I . . ."

"Your what?"

"Wife!" He looked at me as if he were surprised I didn't know. He was putting it on, of course, and he said immediately: "Oh, I guess you wouldn't know, would you? I married Emily just before I left Crook City."

"Married . . . Emily?"

I must have sounded as if I were an idiot. I looked like one, too, I guess, with my mouth hanging open. I just couldn't quite grasp what he was saying. I had liked Emily Durling, and there were a lot of good things I could have said about her, but I had trouble picturing a man, especially Jake Murdock, actually marrying her.

"Yes, Emily," he said impatiently. "I told her I'd send for her as soon as I had built a good house, but she'll come when she hears what I've done. Now there is a chore I want you to do for me. It ain't a pleasant one, but you can handle it better'n me."

He laid his pipe on the table and dug a twenty dollar gold piece out of his pocket and handed it to me. "I want you to harness up the team and take Ellie to the reservation. Give her that. She won't need any money when she gets there, but I want her to have it. Tell her to take all her clothes and whatever quilts she'll need." He couldn't look at me any more. He got up and jammed his hands down hard into his pockets, and added: "Tell her I appreciate her working for me as long as she did."

I stood there, staring at him, frozen inside and not breathing much, and all the time I was thinking this was what I knew was going to happen. But now that it was happening, I couldn't believe it, at least not the way it was happening, with Murdock pushing his dirty work off on me. But he was right on one thing. I could handle it better than he could.

"I know this is bad weather to start out in," he said, "but the sooner she can pack up the better. Oh, yes, I don't expect you to do this for nothing. I'll pay you for your time."

"Jake, you owe Charley Three Horses some wages," I said, my voice sounding strange to me. I had never felt this way before, as if I were standing apart from myself and watching Murdock and me carry on a conversation.

"I'll pay him," he said impatiently.

"Ellie has a bill at Galt's store," I said. "She had to buy supplies for herself and Charley Three Horses."

"I'll pay that, too," he said, his tone still sharp with impatience.

"She will never believe me," I said. "Get a piece of paper and write out what you want her to do."

At first he objected. When I stood there for several seconds not saying anything, but just looking at him, he turned around and left the kitchen. He came back in about five minutes and handed me a folded piece of paper. I took it and shoved it into my pocket.

"You promised to marry Ellie," I said.

"Oh, hell." He dismissed the promise with a careless gesture. "Ellie's a smart girl. She knew I didn't mean it. She knows that a white man never marries a 'breed."

I put on my hat and coat. There was a lot I wanted to tell him, a hell of a lot, but most of it would have been a waste of time and wind. Besides, I think he knew exactly what he was and what he was doing without me spelling it out for him, but I was going to spell some of it out for him anyway.

I walked to the back door, and then I turned and looked at him. I said: "We've been through a lot together, Jake, in the few months we've known each other. You saved my life last spring and I saved yours when I got you into Crook City. Emily said you wouldn't have made it if you'd been a little later getting to her house."

"Well?"

"I just wanted you to know that our debts are balanced," I said. "I also want you to know something I think you already know. Besides being a son-of-a-bitch and a coward for not telling Ellie yourself, you are a god-damned fool."

His big fists knotted and his face turned red, and then almost purple. He started for me, then stopped when I held up my left hand and dropped my right to the butt of my gun. "I'm not a big man," I said, "and I never was much good with my fists, so I never allow a man to lay a hand on me. If you try it, I'll shoot your head off."

He stopped about ten feet from me, a pulse hammering in his forehead. I went out, slamming the door behind me, and walked around the house to Sundown. I mounted and headed back, facing into the wind, and I wondered how I was ever going to tell Ellie what I had to tell her.

Chapter Nineteen

When I got back to the JM, I led Sundown into his stall and stripped off the saddle, and then spent more time than I needed to just rubbing him down. The truth was I hated like hell to go into the house and tell Ellie.

Sure, I'd known this was coming and I'd be around to look after Ellie, but I'd never dreamed that Murdock was too big a coward to tell her himself, and I'd wind up doing the dirty job he should have done.

When I couldn't find anything else to do in the barn, I went to the house, knocked the snow off my boots, and went in. Ellie had the coffee pot on the stove. She poured a cup for me and brought it to me, smiling in that nice way she had that made me love her all the more and mentally call Jake a bigger fool than ever.

"I thought you never were coming in," she said. "Where in the world have you been? I saw you talk to Rand, then you saddled up and rode out without saying a word to me about where you were going."

"I guess I should have." I sat down at the table and motioned for her to sit down. "Get yourself a cup of coffee and get ready to listen to me. It's going to be a shock."

She looked at me questioningly, then she got a cup, filled it with coffee, and sat down across the table from me. Maybe she sensed what was coming. I don't know. I had the damnedest feeling as if I'd known for a long time that something bad was going to happen and now it had.

The funny thing was that through all that long time I had kept hoping it wouldn't happen although I knew it would. I guess that doesn't make much sense, but what Murdock was doing didn't make any sense.

I took a long breath. I knew there wasn't any sense in beating around the bush. The sooner I got it over with, the better. If you've got to stick a knife into a person, there isn't any use looking for a spot where it wouldn't hurt. I knew I wouldn't find it.

"Rand told me Jake was at his place," I said, "and he wanted to see me. That's why I rode over there. He feels fine except that he's still a little thin. He's bought Rand's spread and he's going to make it the JM headquarters. He's going to buy a big herd and hire a crew. Sometime this winter he'll build a bunkhouse. He married Emily Durling and he wants me to take you to the reservation right away."

I stuck the knife into her, all right. I stuck it and gave it a few twists. I might just as well have hit her on the head with a club. She just sat there staring at me while her coffee got cold, staring at me as if she were in a daze. She didn't have any more expression on her face than there was on the wall of that room. Sure, I could have given it to her one thing at a time, but I don't think it would have made any difference.

"He said he appreciated you working for him as long as you did," I went on. "He promised to pay the bill at Galt's store for the supplies you bought this summer." I dug around in my pocket until I found the gold coin he gave me and laid it in front of her. "He said he wanted you to have that."

She acted as if she didn't see it or know it was there. One minute passed, maybe two, maybe five. I don't know, but it seemed like an hour. I didn't know whether I should say anything more or not because I couldn't tell whether she was capable of hearing what I had to say. So I waited. All of a sudden she picked up the gold piece and threw it across the room as hard as she could, and laughed.

"Twenty dollars for four years' work," she said. "I'll take his appreciation and let it go at that." She snatched up her cup and gulped the coffee, then set the empty cup down. "When are we starting for the reservation? You said for me not to think of myself as a squaw, but I guess I'll be a squaw whether I want to be one or not."

I shook my head. "You don't have to go back to the reservation. Why do you think I bought that house from Galt?"

"I don't know," she said. "You never told me."

"Well, I'll tell you now. I bought it for you to live in. You told me you wouldn't go back to the reservation and there is nothing Jake can do to make you go. I can't live with you all the time, but I can see you've got a house to live in, and I'll ask Galt to give you credit for anything you need. There's a bed and a stove in the house, and I figure we can take enough from here to get started."

She didn't cry. Her voice didn't even tremble when she said: "All right. This is a bad day to move, but I guess we can do it. You harness up the team and hook up the wagon and pull around to the door. We'd better get started."

I got up and crossed the room to where she had thrown the gold piece. I picked it up and dropped it in my pocket, then put on my sheepskin and hat and went outside.

It was a day I'll never forget. We simply piled stuff in the bed of the wagon—Ellie's clothes, bedding, groceries, most of the furniture, and enough wood to last a week or so, and then I threw a canvas over the load. Ellie put on her heavy coat and cap and for a moment stood looking around the stripped room. Then she walked out and got into the wagon seat. She still hadn't shed a tear.

We were cold by the time we got to Galt City, and of course some of the stuff was wet, but not badly. It was a dry snow and not much had piled up on the ground. Most of it was still headed for Nebraska. I built a fire first thing, then Ellie made the bed, and the next thing I knew Slim Galt had come over from the store.

"Can I help?" he asked.

"You sure can," I said, "but I think you'd better know a few things first. Jake Murdock's back and wants Ellie off his place. Seems like he got married and he'll be sending for his wife right away."

"I know about that," he said. "Carl Rand told me.

He bought one of the other houses, so the population of Galt City is increasing by leaps and bounds."

"Well, what you don't know is that Ellie will be living here as long as she wants to stay," I said. "I'll be with her till she gets straightened around, then I'll go somewhere. I don't know where, but I want to find work, and there isn't any for me here. We're not married. I hope we will be, but we're not now."

He looked at me and then at Ellie and back to me as if he were absolutely astonished. He said: "My God, Lang, what's the matter with you? I'm not your conscience or your judge. It ain't none of my business, either way."

Ellie sighed. "Thank you, Mister Galt."

"Well, then, if we're welcome in Galt City," I said, "there are a few other minor items. Murdock has agreed to pay Ellie's bill that she owes you, but from now on I'll be responsible for what she buys. I may end up a long way from here and I want to know she's being taken care of."

Galt laughed softly. "You're a worrier, Lang. Of course, I'll give her credit. More than that, Mirandy will visit with her and be glad she's here. She's been right down lonesome this summer, Mirandy has."

"Have you got any lumber to sell?" I asked.

"That I do," he said, "and more on the way from Cheyenne. Rand is starting to build his saloon as soon as the weather clears. I'm a purty fair carpenter myself. So's my boy Jim. By spring I intend to have several business buildings on Main Street finished and ready to move into. We need a hotel and a livery stable and I'm hoping we can get a newspaper started." He spread his hands and laughed like a schoolboy. "The Galt City *Weekly Bugle*. How's that?"

I laughed, too, and Ellie managed a grin. I said: "What I had in mind was a small barn on the back of the lot. I'll take the wagon back tonight and fetch my saddle horse. Until I get a barn put up, I'll want to keep my horse in yours."

"Of course," he agreed. "Now, if that's all, let's carry the rest of your stuff inside."

As soon as we were done, I drove back to the JM, unhooked and stripped the harness off the team, and saddled Sundown. I intended to get off Murdock's land and stay off. From this day on I wanted no part of Jake Murdock.

I felt queerly about the whole business because I couldn't get out of my mind the fact that Murdock had saved my life. We had been through a lot together this last summer, and I considered him a friend. I'd never had a friend, not the way Murdock and I had been, but now that was past. I hated the bastard, and, if he pushed me or made things tough for Ellie, I'd kill him. I was sure of it.

By the time I got back to Galt City, Ellie had things put away, enough so the house seemed livable. It was tight, the stove was a good one, and we were comfortable and warm. I put Sundown in Galt's barn and waded back through the snow, about six inches now, and sat and watched Ellie cook supper.

As soon as we finished and Ellie had done the dishes, she yawned and said: "Let's go to bed. I'm tired."

"It's been a tough day," I said.

When we were in bed and the covers over us and

the darkness all around us, Ellie snuggled close to me. She whispered: "Love me, Bill. Love me hard. I'm empty inside. I've got to have something to hold to."

Later, just before we dropped off to sleep, I said: "Will you marry me now, Ellie?"

"No," she whispered. "Don't ask me why. I . . . I just can't."

I guess I expected that, although I'm not sure I really understood. I wasn't sure she did, either. I thought she needed a little time to get over everything that had happened today, and that, when enough time had passed, she would marry me. I was wrong. It took more time than I had expected, much, much more.

Chapter Twenty

I stayed in Galt City for one week. I hired young Jim Galt to help me build the barn and found that he was handier with tools than I was. When we finished, we bought a couple of loads of hay and half a dozen sacks of oats, and I told Ellie that I'd buy her a horse if she wanted one so she wouldn't have to depend on the Galts if she decided to go anywhere. Or I could leave Sundown, but she said no, she wasn't going anywhere. So then I told her she could buy a horse from Galt later on if she decided she did want one.

The morning I left I stopped at the store. "Murdock told me to take Ellie to the reservation," I said to Galt, "but I didn't because she didn't want to go. There's not a damned thing he can do to make her go, but he's a bull-headed man and he may make trouble. I'd like for you to look out for her as much as you can."

Galt's mouth tightened up. He said: "I don't mind

GET
4 FREE BOOKS!

You can have the best Westerns delivered to your door for less than what you'd pay in a bookstore or online. Sign up for one of our book clubs today, and we'll send you 4 FREE* BOOKS, worth $23.96, just for trying it out...with no obligation to buy, ever!

Authors include classic writers such as
LOUIS L'AMOUR, MAX BRAND, ZANE GREY
and more; PLUS new authors such as
COTTON SMITH, TIM CHAMPLIN, JOHNNY D. BOGGS
and others.

As a book club member you also receive the following special benefits:
- 30% OFF all orders through our website & telecenter!
- Exclusive access to special discounts!
- Convenient home delivery and 10 days to return any books you don't want to keep.

There is no minimum number of books to buy,
and you may cancel membership at any time.
See back to sign up!

*Please include $2.00 for shipping and handling.

YES!

Sign me up for the Leisure Western Book Club and send my FOUR FREE BOOKS! If I choose to stay in the club, I will pay only $14.00* each month, a savings of $9.96!

NAME: _____

ADDRESS: _____

_____

TELEPHONE: _____

E-MAIL: _____

☐ I WANT TO PAY BY CREDIT CARD.

☐ VISA   ☐ MasterCard.   ☐ DISCOVER

ACCOUNT #: _____

EXPIRATION DATE: _____

SIGNATURE: _____

Send this card along with $2.00 shipping & handling to:

**Leisure Western Book Club
1 Mechanic Street
Norwalk, CT 06850-3431**

Or fax (must include credit card information!) to: 610.995.9274.
You can also sign up online at www.dorchesterpub.com.

*Plus $2.00 for shipping. Offer open to residents of the U.S. and Canada only.
Canadian residents please call 1.800.481.9191 for pricing information.
If under 18, a parent or guardian must sign. Terms, prices and conditions subject to change. Subscription subject
to acceptance. Dorchester Publishing reserves the right to reject any order or cancel any subscription.

JOIN NOW!

telling you, Lang, that I wish you were staying here, but Jim and me can shoot. I reckon Carl Rand can, too. If it comes to that, I suppose Ellie can do her share of fighting."

I nodded. "She can, but she's got a kind of a funny feeling about Murdock. She lived with him for four years, you know."

"Well, she sure don't owe him nothing, after the way he throwed her out. You know, I'm glad you're on our side instead of Murdock's." He wagged a forefinger at me. "You ain't gonna regret it, neither. Before you're done, them lots you bought for a song are gonna make you rich."

"I hope so," I said, and didn't believe a word of it. I'd make a profit, all right, but getting rich was something else. "I'll try to get back at Christmas or sooner if I don't end up too far away."

We shook hands, and he said: "Ellie's gonna need you."

I didn't know what he meant. Not then. I rode to Cheyenne and started looking for a lawman's job of some kind, figuring I could be a deputy out of the sheriff's office, or maybe a U.S. marshal. The only skill I had was with a gun, and it seemed stupid not to make use of it.

I didn't have any luck, though. I even rode out to Fort D.A. Russell and talked to some of the officers who had been with Crook and knew me, but they couldn't help.

In the end I took a job riding shotgun on the stage between Cheyenne and the Black Hills. I passed within a few miles of Galt City every trip I made and I wished I could see Ellie and find out what was happening. I wondered if Rand had his saloon up and what Galt had done about the buildings he was planning to put up on Main Street.

I didn't get back to Galt City until a couple of days before Christmas. I rode in from Cheyenne late in the afternoon with an inch of snow on the ground. The sun was a fireball just above the Laramie range in an absolutely clear blue sky. The air was cold, but it didn't seem too cold because there wasn't any wind.

As I rode into town, I saw it actually had begun to look like a town. Rand had his saloon finished and Galt had built three small buildings that would do as offices for lawyers or doctors and might even be big enough for a print shop.

Then I turned off Main Street and saw Ellie carrying a bucket of water from the well back of the store. I yelled and she yelled when she saw who it was. She set the bucket on the ground and ran toward me. I reined up and stepped down and took her into my arms.

I'd had the impression she had been running awkwardly and that she looked out of proportion, but it still took me a little while to grasp fully the idea that her belly was swollen because she was going to have a baby.

I was naïve about anything like that. I'd never been around pregnant women. In fact, I'd never seen many, or at least I hadn't noticed them, and, after Ellie had lived with Murdock for four years and hadn't got knocked up, I never even considered the possibility that she would now.

It hit me so hard that I didn't, or couldn't, say a

word all the way to the house. I led Sundown to the front door and carried the bucket inside and set it on the table, then I looked at her. She looked at me and didn't say anything, but she was worried. I could see that, and I thought she was going to start to cry. She didn't, though. She just stood there swallowing and looking at me.

"Is it mine?" I asked.

She backed up, a hand coming to her throat. She shook her head. "It's Jake's." She bit her lower lip, then she blurted: "I wouldn't be this big if it was yours. Not in two or three months. It happened just before Jake left in May."

"Does he know?"

She shook her head again. "No use to tell him. He wouldn't believe it was his. Anyhow, he's married. He couldn't do anything for me now." Then she did begin to cry. She said between sobs: "What are you going to do? Are you going to leave me?"

"No, of course not," I said. "Now you'll have to marry me."

She turned away and walked to a window and looked outside. I went to her and put an arm around her. I said: "I guess you knew before I left?"

"Yes, I knew," she said, "and the Galts knew, but I couldn't tell you. I didn't know what you'd do or think. I was afraid you wouldn't come back."

I thought about it a minute and I guess that was when I began to hate Jake Murdock. Oh, I had hated him before, a little bit at a time. For instance, when he told me to take Ellie to the reservation and had sent a lousy twenty-dollar gold piece to her with a righteous statement that he wanted her to have it and I was to tell her he appreciated her working for him. *She won't need any money when she gets to the reservation,* he had said.

Now it was different. I hated him in a way I had never hated any man before. I stood there with my arm around Ellie, loving her more than ever and knowing I'd marry her any time she'd have me, and knowing that with Murdock it wouldn't have made any difference whether he had married Emily Durling or not. If it hadn't been Emily, it would have been some other white woman. Even if he had known when he'd left last May that Ellie was carrying his child, he still wouldn't have married her. He'd have shipped her off to the reservation just the same.

After a long time, I said: "I am back, Ellie. Nothing's changed. I still want to marry you."

She took a deep breath. "I've got to wait, Bill. I've got to wait until after the baby comes."

I didn't argue with her. I figured that her reason, whatever it might be, was a good one. To her, anyway. I could wait, too.

In the morning I went over to the store and asked Galt whether Murdock had made any trouble. "Yes and no," he said. "He tried. It was a couple of weeks after you left. His wife had got here and he brought her to the store to shop. He went across the street to talk to Rand who was working on his building. I guess Murdock hadn't heard Ellie was here until Rand mentioned it. He got white in the face, Rand said, and turned around and started for your house. Rand came tearing over here after me. We took revolvers and followed him. He was inside the house yelling at Ellie and telling her she had to go back to the reservation. We let him see the business ends of our Forty-Fives and told him to let her alone. He got his wife out of the store and he hasn't been back since."

I stood there listening, and all the time I was wondering if I ought to go see him. The chances were I'd kill him if I did and I didn't want to do that. He'd probably let her alone now, so I decided to let it ride.

"Thanks," I said. "I don't suppose he'll show up here again."

Galt laughed. "No, sir. I don't think a team of wild horses could pull him back into Galt City."

"I'm leaving again in a couple of days," I said. "Ellie still won't marry me. I won't be back till spring unless something happens to bring me back. You think she'll be all right?"

"She'll be fine," he said. "Mirandy is as good as a doctor when it comes to delivering babies. Ellie won't have any trouble. Having a little Indian blood is a help."

"I'll settle up with you for what Ellie's bought," I said. "I'll do the same when I get back. Have Jim see that she has plenty of wood and coal."

He got a little huffy then. "Damn it, Bill, I wish you'd quit worrying about her. I told you we'd look out for her. And as far as settling up is concerned, wait till you get back. I hope you'll live here, come spring. This place is going to be busting at the seams as soon as the weather clears and we'll need you."

"Why me?"

"We'll need a cold, tough customer for a deputy sheriff," he said. "We're going to have a crowd of people flocking in. We'll have a construction camp on the flat and you always get a bunch of hardcases coming into a country like this when things are booming. I'll see that you get a deputy's badge and I'll also see that you are paid more than the stage company is paying you."

"I think I'd like that," I said.

I turned to leave, but he stopped me with: "Bill, do you want to sell your lots on Main Street?"

"No," I said. "Why?"

"I should have held 'em," he said. "I can give you five hundred dollars apiece. That's five hundred percent profit."

"Not enough," I said. "You told me they'd make me rich. I'll wait till they do."

I felt pretty good about it when I rode south the day after Christmas. If I could make 500 percent after owning those lots two or three months, what could I do after six months? Or a year?

I wasn't any kind of a businessman, and I certainly had never had any ambition to be rich the way Murdock had, but it would be kind of nice to have enough money to know you didn't have to work unless you wanted to or enough to do what you wanted to when you wanted to. It would be nice for Ellie, too. She deserved it.

Chapter Twenty-One

As soon as the weather cleared in the spring, I began hearing a lot about Galt City and the irrigation project. Slim Galt had run ads in the Cheyenne newspapers offering town lots for sale and inviting settlers to take up land so they would be ready to start raising crops as soon as the water was available. On every trip I made to the Black Hills, the stage would pass a dozen or more heavily loaded freight wagons between Cheyenne and the Galt City junction.

I'd had a letter from Ellie in March saying the baby was born the 1st of the month, a big, healthy boy she had named Mick. I was about ready to quit my job early in June when I had a letter from Galt asking me to come back and again offering to buy my lots. The town was booming, he said, and it was the time to sell. The deputy's star was waiting to be pinned on me, and, if I didn't get there in a week or so, he'd have to look for someone else.

One more trip to the Black Hills, and, when I returned to Cheyenne, the company had a replacement for me. I saddled Sundown and headed north to Galt City. Hearing what I had about the town, and even with the information Galt's letter had given me, I still was unprepared for what I saw. Somehow it didn't seem physically possible for any place to grow this way in less than six months.

The only vacant lots on Main Street were the ones I owned. There were two new saloons, a hotel, a livery stable, a blacksmith shop, another general store, a drugstore, a jewelry store, and several small buildings that housed all kinds of offices from those of real estate agents and land locaters to that of the Galt Valley Land Development Company.

When I reached the corner, I saw that there was a jail across a side street, with an office in front for the town marshal. Boardwalks were laid out on both sides of Main Street, and hitch racks were put up in front of every business building. But what surprised me the most was the crowd of people on the street and the number of horses and rigs of all kinds at the hitch rails. It seemed to me I could sense the hustle and bustle of a boom town just from riding down the middle of the street.

I was surprised, too, by the amount of building that had been done on the back streets. The only vacant lots for about two blocks on Lincoln Street were the ones I owned. Some of the houses were one-room shacks that would soon be rebuilt or added to, but others were good, permanent dwellings, most of them painted white with green or red or blue trim, and many with white picket fences around their yards.

As I dismounted in front of the house, I saw a

schoolhouse farther down the street, and a church on beyond it. To me it was simply unbelievable that a town could mushroom out of the Wyoming prairie when there had been nothing here a year ago except sagebrush and grass.

Ellie ran out of the house before I was halfway to the front door. "Bill!" she screamed, and ran into my arms. I hugged and kissed her, and then pushed her back and looked at her. She was as slim and attractive as ever. Having a baby hadn't hurt her looks and I told her so.

She smiled at me, a little trembling upturn at the corners of her mouth. She said: "Aren't you going to stay here now and live with me?"

"I figured I would," I said. "Galt wrote that I had a job waiting for me."

"He told me that, too," she said. "He wants you to come and see him as soon as you get here. You'll find him in the company office. Mirandy and Jim are running the store with some hired help." She hesitated, and then added slowly: "I could have had a job in the store if I didn't have to stay home with Mick."

"You don't have to work," I said. "I'll take care of you."

"I know you will," she said. "Slim says you're a rich man. He's got a buyer who's been after him to get hold of you, but he kept saying you'd be here pretty soon and he could make the deal with you."

I still had my hands on her shoulders and I wanted to say something about getting married, but then I thought I'd asked her so many times and she hadn't wanted to that there wasn't any sense in asking her again. I think she must have read my mind.

"I guess marriage is a big thing to white women," she said, looking straight at me, "but it isn't to me. We couldn't love each other any more if we were married than we do right now." She hesitated, then she said: "Slim says you're going to be a big man in this community and we ought to tell folks we're married now. Nobody would know the difference. He says it would look better to the new people who don't know all that's happened." She hesitated again, and then she cleared her throat and blurted: "Bill, I'm not sure if I've done the right thing or not, but I've been telling people I'm Missus Lang and everybody thinks you're Mick's father."

I grinned. The whole thing struck me kind of funny. It didn't and hadn't made any difference to me whether we were married or not. I just thought it would to Ellie because that's the way women are, but she'd just made it plain she didn't care one way or the other.

I guess she'd had enough Indian upbringing that she could see through the sham and hypocrisy of the white civilization. To her, standing in front of a preacher and mumbling a few words and having him preach a few words at us wasn't what was really important.

"All right, Missus Lang," I said. "All I want is you."

She put her hands on my arms and gripped me as hard as she could. She said: "Bill, you've had me for a long time. You didn't know it, I guess, but you had me right from the first."

"I thought it was Jake," I said.

"It was," she agreed, "but that was because I belonged to him. He had given me a home. If it hadn't been for him, I would have been sent back to the reservation. I couldn't have stood it, not after living the way I had. I owed everything to him and I tried to please him to pay him back, but it was different when you came along. It was kind of like God had sent you to me."

I'd never thought about it that way. She seldom mentioned God and I didn't really know what she believed. I was sure she didn't believe the way the Sioux did, but I didn't think she believed the way the preacher did who had taken her from the reservation, either.

"Well, let's go have a look at Mick," I said.

She stepped back, her face suddenly shadowed by fear. I didn't know what was wrong until I went into the house with her. The baby was lying on the bed covered by a blanket. She pulled the blanket off him. He was asleep, almost naked, the biggest, healthiest-looking baby I ever saw who was only about three months old. He was just as brown-skinned as Charley Three Horses.

I don't know of anything that could have surprised me more. I seldom thought of Ellie being one-quarter Sioux, as light-skinned as she was. The baby, of course, would be only one-eighth Indian. I had assumed he'd be even lighter-skinned than Ellie, but I had been a fool to assume anything of the sort. I knew how this kind of thing worked, and I should have been prepared. But I wasn't.

Then I noticed something else, something I would have noticed right away if I hadn't been hit so hard by the baby's dark skin. He had black hair, which was to be expected, and his eyes would be brown. Murdock had gray eyes and hair that was as reddish brown as his mustache, but the part that hit me now was that Mick was a small copy of Murdock. He had the same square head and the same features even to the cleft that dented the bottom middle of his wide chin.

I looked at Ellie. She was staring at me, her face as pale as I had ever seen it. She whispered: "Now you know why I didn't want to marry you. I was afraid he might look like that. Everybody will know when they see him that I'm a half-breed and maybe that will hurt you. I want you to be free to leave me any time you want to."

"I'll never want to leave you," I said. "Now quit worrying."

I turned around and walked out of the house. I put Sundown in the barn and stripped off the saddle. I watered and fed him, and rubbed him down, then I filled my pipe and hunkered down in front of the barn and smoked until the tobacco was gone.

No amount of rolling this around in my mind was going to change anything. I didn't care about the baby being dark or folks saying they didn't know Ellie was a half-breed until they looked at her baby. The one point that stuck in my craw was the simple fact that I didn't want to raise Jake's kid.

Maybe it was just pride, but, by God, I couldn't stand for folks looking at Mick and then at me, and finally at Jake Murdock, and saying behind my back that Murdock had got to Ellie before I had.

But there was nothing that was going to make me give up Ellie, and no man in his sane mind would ask a woman to give her baby away. So there it was,

as plain as the big Murdock nose on the kid's face.
I'd raise the baby as if he were mine.

I went into the house and told Ellie, but there was
one thing I didn't tell her. I was going to let Murdock know Mick was his child.

Chapter Twenty-Two

I went to the office of the Galt Valley Land Development Company the first thing after breakfast the following morning. Slim Galt was behind his desk in his private office. He rushed out as soon as he heard me ask for him and shook hands as if I were governor; then he invited me to come on back into his office.

Prosperity had come to Slim Galt. He had a fat cigar clamped between his teeth in one corner of his mouth; he wore a white shirt and black string tie and a brown broadcloth suit, but it took more than clothes to change Galt's country appearance. He had the same gangling, homely look about him that had impressed me the first time I'd seen him.

I still had the feeling that he was about the least likely-looking promoter I had ever seen in my life, but of course I realized that it was this very quality that would appeal to the settlers and make them trust him.

In all the years I knew Slim Galt, he never cheated

me, and I never knew him to cheat the men he dealt
with, and yet I was never sure whether the feeling of
human warmth that seemed to flow out of him was
put on or was sincere. Somehow it seemed too good
to be true, but I'll admit I never had any reason to
doubt him.

He motioned me toward a chair and offered me a
cigar, and said: "I'm sure glad you're back, Bill. Now
are you going to stay?"

I nodded. "If I've got that job you offered me."

"You sure have," he said. "I've made arrangements for you to be appointed deputy sheriff. The
job will pay you one hundred dollars a month.
We've got a jail built just waiting for you. The star's
over at the jail in the top drawer of your desk. You'll
have to patrol the flat and check at the construction
camp every day. Saturday nights these boys will
come to town and raise hell and you'll have to keep
the lid on."

He made a half turn in his swivel chair and
pointed at a map of Galt City that was tacked to the
wall. "We aren't incorporated yet, but we will be.
Meanwhile, I have pledges from ten businessmen
for each of them to throw ten dollars into the hat for
your salary as town marshal until we can raise it by
taxes. The most important thing is for us to keep order here in town if we're going to get settlers on the
land and the right kind of permanent business people in town."

He ran a finger to the end of Main Street. "We've
got two whorehouses right here. That's enough. If
more come, we'll work some shenanigan to run 'em
out . . . maybe set the license fee so high they can't
afford to operate here. Personally I don't believe in

'em and I don't want 'em in town, but as long as we've got the construction men on the flat, I guess we need 'em."

"If you don't have them in town," I said, "you'll have hog ranches out in the country like they've got around Fort Laramie. It's better to have them here so you can keep them under some sort of supervision."

He shrugged, and said a little impatiently: "I know the argument and it might be right. Well, now, besides that we've got saloons. There's a certain amount of gambling going on in all of them. We've had some brawls and we'll have some more. We haven't had any killings, but we will. Most of the people coming in are good, law-abiding, family-type folks, but there are always some riff-raff. I want you to make it hard on them so they won't stay."

"Oh, come off of it, Slim," I said. "You know that a boom town draws men like that. You can't keep 'em out."

"I know." He spread his hands. "But we won't always be a boom town. If we can keep the violence down, it will help bring in the right kind of settlers and businessmen who will settle down. In the long run, it'll make for a peaceful, prosperous community."

"It'll work that way," I agreed. "I think it always works that way."

He leaned back in his chair and stared at the ceiling and chewed on his cigar. He said: "I hope so." He tipped his chair forward and added: "I'll take you around and introduce you to the businessmen in town. How soon can you go to work?"

I didn't answer immediately. There was something I wanted to know and I'd been reluctant to ask

Ellie about it. I said: "Tell me about Emily and Jake Murdock and the JM, and how many other big outfits are in the country now."

"It'd take the morning to tell you all about them," he said, "but it is part of our problem. At least a dozen big herds have been brought in since the first of the year, so we'll have a ranch country and a farm community side-by-side, and that's like trying to mix oil and water."

"I don't suppose the cowboys come into town much," I said.

"Well, not much," he admitted. "As a matter of fact, we haven't encouraged them. We don't have many farmers on the flat yet, but they're beginning to come. We figure that the cowboys will make trouble and we can get along without their business."

"Murdock?"

"Oh, he never comes to town and he won't let his hands come in, either. He's hired an eight-man crew including a gun slick named Smoke Bunker, though why he needs a gunman is more'n I know. About two weeks ago he drove in a herd of about two thousand head, mostly young stuff."

"He was going to build a bunkhouse," I said. "Did he do it?"

Galt grinned. "Yes, sir, he done it. Also a cook shack and he's hired a Chinese cook." He hesitated, then he said: "There is one thing I'd better tell you. It happened more'n a month ago. First of May, I think it was, but you still may have to investigate it. You knew Emily's brother, the hunchback?"

I nodded. "He was in Crook City when I was there."

"He was strictly no good as far as I could tell. He

hated Murdock and he didn't mind telling you, if he could buttonhole you on the street or in a saloon. He'd go into a long speech about Murdock being a son-of-a-bitch and how his sister Emily robbed him of half of the family inheritance and how he was gonna get his half by hook or crook. He was always begging drinks and trying to gamble with nothing better'n his I.O.U. Murdock and Emily ran an ad in the *Bugle* saying they wouldn't be responsible for his debts, so everybody was careful about giving him credit."

Galt got up and walked to the window. I wondered what had happened because it was plain enough he was upset about it.

"Well, one night Carl Rand got him drunk," Galt went on. "He done it on purpose because he kept telling me that Murdock didn't have enough money to buy a big herd and hire a crew and do all the building he done this winter. We could guess where he got the money, but we didn't know. For some reason Carl had to know, so he kept pushing the drinks at Lacey. Purty soon Lacey's tongue got oiled up. He claimed it was a sort of deal between Murdock and Emily when they were in Crook City. She wanted a husband and a home, and he wanted a big spread, and they could do that for each other. Lacey claimed that Murdock had almost busted Emily with his buying and building and big scheming."

I wasn't surprised. I don't suppose it was quite that cut and dried, but I recalled enough of my conversation with Emily last summer to believe something like that had happened.

"It was three, four days before the end of April," Galt said. "The story is all over town, and, even though Murdock and Emily never came to town, I figure they must have heard it. Lacey came back to Rand's Bar the evening of May 1st. He had money that night. Purty soon he got drunk and he was a good fellow, buying drinks for everybody. Along 'bout midnight he started home, but he was so drunk he fell off his horse right out in the street. Somebody helped him back on and he started out again, but he never got home. The next morning he was found halfway between here and the JM, all bunged up, including a broken neck. Everybody supposed he fell off his horse, but there's talk that Murdock met him and broke his neck for him."

"Could have been that way," I said, "but there's no use for me to investigate something that happened more than a month ago."

Galt shrugged. "I thought you ought to know in case it does come up."

"I'll answer your question now," I said. "I'll go to work in the morning. I'm going out to the JM today to see Jake."

"Don't do that," Galt said sharply. "You won't be welcome. That JM crew is a salty outfit. It ain't just the gun slick, Bunker. They're all a bunch of hardcases."

"It's more reason for me to go." I rose. "Now let's go meet my bosses."

Galt took a black derby off a nail and clapped it on his head. It didn't seem to fit his character any more than the broadcloth suit and the white shirt and the string tie, but it didn't really change anything except to hide the bald part of his head. "We'll look at the jail first," Galt said.

We went out and across the side street to the office and jail. It was adequate, I thought. Handcuffs. A gun rack with half a dozen rifles and a double-barreled shotgun. A desk with a drawer half full of Reward dodgers and several boxes of shells. One big cell in the back half.

"What are the chances of making a new county up here someday?" I asked.

"Good," he said. "We've talked about it, but it'll be ten years yet, maybe more."

He led the way back across the side street and started with the first office next to the land company. It belonged to a real estate agent named Jason P. Whipple, a sharpshooter if I ever saw one.

Whipple was a slender, dapper man with a hairline mustache, curly hair that was so carefully combed it seemed that each hair was in its exact place, and a gold chain across his vest. When he shook hands, his palm was soft and a little moist. I instinctively didn't like him, but I certainly liked what he said.

"I'm very happy to meet you, Mister Lang," he said. "I want to buy your lots. I'll give you one thousand dollars for the residential lots on Lincoln Street, and two thousand for your business lots."

I blinked and wondered if I had heard right. I looked at Galt, remembering he had told me they would make me rich. If I could still figure, and I wasn't sure I could after what Whipple had just said, it looked as if I'd get $15,000 for the ten lots. I would, of course, hold out the lot on which we lived.

"I don't know," I said, and kept looking at Galt.

He laughed softly. "I'll give you some advice, Bill, and you may hate me if you take it. If I were you, I'd sell except for your corner lot on Main Street. Hang onto it. Just one thing. Remember Jason here is gambling on values going up. If you sell, you're gambling on them being at their peak now.

If I held onto the corner lot, I'd still get $13,000. I said: "I'll take it except for the corner lot."

Afterward, I walked along the street with Galt and met the rest of the businessmen, but I was in such a daze that I didn't remember half of them by noon. $13,000! All I could think of was that if I lived a long and prosperous life, I never expected to have that much. Galt had been right. Those lots had made me rich.

Chapter Twenty-Three

I rode out to the JM late in the afternoon, figuring it was the best time to catch Murdock. All the way out there I wondered what I'd say to him and what would happen. Actually I couldn't even pin down in my own mind why I wanted to see him.

It was just that we hadn't seen each other since I had failed to take Ellie to the reservation. Now that I was going to live in Galt City, a few miles from the JM, I figured I'd better give him a chance to do whatever he wanted to.

If he didn't do anything, then there was nothing to worry about. If he did, we'd get it over with and be done with it. Besides, I was wearing my deputy's star. I figured he'd better know about that, too.

When I reined up in front of the big, ugly house that Carl Rand had built, I told myself that there wasn't any doubt about a woman living here. There were white curtains at the windows, a patch of grass in front along with a row of small cottonwoods that had been moved from the Chug, and some green vines growing up a trellis beside the front door.

I didn't see any activity around the corrals or barn, so I figured Jake hadn't ridden in yet. I knocked, and a moment later Emily came out of the back of the house. She stared at me a moment, then cried—"Bill Lang!"—and just sort of jumped at me. She hugged me and patted me on the back, and then she said: "Bill, I've been wondering why you hadn't come out to see us."

"I just got here," I said. "I was in town at Christmas, but that was only for a day or two."

"Come in, come in," she said. "The coffee pot's on the stove. That's about the first thing I learned when I moved here. If you're going to be a good ranch wife, never, never let the coffee pot go dry."

I laughed and followed her through the cool gloom of the house into the kitchen. She motioned for me to sit down at the table, then went into the pantry and returned with two cups. She filled them with hot coffee, set one in front of me, and pulled up a chair and sat down across the table from me with the other cup.

"Well, that starvation march of Crook's seems a long time ago, doesn't it?" she said. "Do you still have nightmares about it?"

"No, I've been able to forget it," I answered.

"Jake does pretty well," she said, "but once in a while he'll wake up in the middle of the night yelling that he's starving or he's cold and wet. I shake him and talk to him, and he'll kind of shudder and drop back on the bed."

"He had it tougher than I did," I said.

"I suppose so." She stared at her cup moodily, and then said: "Jake's out on the range with his crew now, but he'll be in any time."

I filled my pipe and looked at her, but she was staring at her cup and I doubt that she was aware of my scrutiny. She hadn't changed. That is, she was still big and kind of homely and all, but there was something about her that was different. I couldn't identify it. I felt it, though, even if I couldn't see it.

"How do you like being a rancher's wife?" I asked.

She shrugged. "It's all right. It's just that I seem to have so much to learn. I'm plain ignorant, but Jake's got what he wants and that's something." She tapped her fingertips on the table and looked at me. Suddenly she smiled. "Bill, I've thought so many times about the week you were in Crook City, and the good talks we had. I had never met a man who was as easy to talk to as you were. I . . . I guess I said some things I shouldn't, but at the time I never dreamed that someday I'd be living near you."

"I won't repeat them," I said. "As a matter of fact, I've forgotten most of them."

She pointed at my star. "What are you, and did you come out here in performance of your duty?"

"I'm a deputy sheriff and town marshal," I answered. "Or will be a town marshal when Galt City is a town. No, I just came out to see you and Jake."

"I'm glad you did," she said. "Is there a doctor in Galt City?"

I nodded. "A Doctor Ross. I just met him this morning."

"If he ever needs a nurse, tell him about me," she

said. "Jake won't like it, but I've got to do something more useful than just keeping house."

"I'm sorry about Lacey," I said.

She didn't say anything for a minute or more, her face turning grave again. Then she said: "Bill, I know what this sounds like and maybe I'm a monster, but I'm glad he's dead. I couldn't do anything with him. He made life miserable for Jake and me both, but I was stuck with him. I didn't know where to send him and there wasn't anyone else to take care of him. I don't know anything about what happens to us after we die, but it'll be better for Lacey, whatever it is."

I nodded. Sure, it did seem to be the wrong thing to say, but I knew how it had been. Then, suddenly, I knew something else, or thought I did. It had been Emily, not Jake, who had met Lacey on the way back to the JM and killed him. I couldn't prove it, of course, and I don't know how I knew, but I was just as certain as if the words had been written out in big, red letters across the top of the table.

There was an awkward moment of silence, then I heard horses and I rose and put my pipe in my pocket. "I guess that's Jake," I said.

"Yes, that'll be Jake," she agreed.

Then I thought I identified what I had sensed about Emily that had eluded me at first. She was living in a hell of guilt because of Lacey; she had married Jake and had come here and given him her money. Lacey's, too, probably, but it hadn't worked out. At least she wasn't happy.

I left the house as Jake and his crew reined up in front of the corral and dismounted. I don't think

Jake recognized Sundown or had any notion I was there until he saw me leave the house, and then he froze, staring at me as if I'd risen from the grave.

"Jake, come here," I said when I was halfway to the corral.

He had said something to his men when he first saw me. I didn't have any idea what it was, but one of them moved away from the others. Jake hadn't changed. He was just as big and square-headed and wide-jawed as ever. Last fall, when he'd told me to take Ellie back to the reservation, he'd been thin, but he'd picked up the pounds he'd lost. It seemed to me he looked exactly as he'd looked more than a year ago the first time I saw him.

I stopped when I was thirty feet or more from Jake. I had glanced at his crew and I had a hunch that Galt had been right in calling these men a salty outfit, but the one who had stepped away from the rest was cut from another bolt of cloth. He was the gunman, Smoke Bunker.

The gunslinger was a barren-faced man, thin-lipped, sharp-nosed, and with a .45 carried low in a tied-down holster the way a professional does. I was too far away to see the color of his eyes, but I had a hunch that, if I'd been close enough, I'd have seen pale blue eyes that were utterly expressionless.

"I want to talk to you, Jake," I said.

"I've got nothing to say to you," he said harshly.

"What I've got to tell you is something you don't want everybody hearing," I said, "so you'd better get a move on."

"Hey, you smell something, boss?" Bunker asked. "I get it every time I see one of them tin stars. Kind o' like skunk, only worse."

"Now you're a big cowman, Jake," I said. "You're hiring cheap killers. That's what it takes to be a big cowman, isn't it?"

"You ought to know," Murdock said.

"That's right," I said. "I've been one, and I've seen plenty of them. I can spot them a mile off. Now get that son-of-a-bitch off my back or I'll blow his brains out."

Bunker snickered. "Try it, friend. Try it."

His right hand hovered over the butt of his gun. He'd be fast, I thought, but not fast enough. You never face a man like that thinking he might be fast enough, or sooner or later you'll run into one who was.

I started to turn toward Bunker. That was all it took. He went for his gun. He had it clear of leather and he was bringing it up fast when I shot him, once in the chest and once in the throat. He never got off a shot. He went back and down, his head making a solid *thunk* against the corral bars as he fell.

When the echoes of those two shots had died, I said: "Now will you come here, Jake?"

His face was dead white. I suppose he hadn't really expected it to go that far. Or maybe he thought I'd get on my horse and ride off. I don't know what he thought, but he came to me, all right, his legs moving as if they were stilts. He was trembling when he reached me.

"The rest of you stand pat," I said, and lowered my voice. "You'd better come and see your boy, Jake. He's a fine, strong baby."

He went back a step, his eyes bugging out of his head, his face turning still whiter, although I hadn't thought that was possible. Spit drooled from the corners of his mouth. He raised a hand and wiped the spit away. He said in little more than a whisper: "You're lying. He's yours."

I shook my head. "No. As a matter of timing, he couldn't be, but you'd have to take my word for that. Or Ellie's. You'll have to see him. No son of mine could have the head shape he's got, or the features, either."

I backed up to Sundown and mounted, my gun still in my hand. I rode away, none of them offering to pull a gun or to follow me.

I had no regrets about killing Smoke Bunker. The world was a better place without him. I should know. I had been very much that same kind of man a year ago last March when I'd ridden north from Trinidad. I still would be if I had never met Ellie.

Chapter Twenty-Four

When I got home, Ellie had supper ready. Charley Three Horses was there, sitting on the porch, holding the baby. I shook hands with him. It was the first time I'd seen him since the day I'd got back from Crook City. Ellie hadn't mentioned him and I hadn't got around to asking about him.

"How are you getting along, Charley?" I asked.

"Good."

Ellie came to the door and said: "Come in and eat." She took the baby from Charley and sat down and began to nurse him. She added: "Charley doesn't get to town very often. I haven't seen him for two months."

Charley said: "Ran out of the grub." He sat down at the table and helped himself to the ham and potatoes and biscuits and began to eat.

He never had been one to talk very much, but he seemed more taciturn than usual tonight. I was curious about him because there weren't many like him in the country any more. New people were coming in and I wondered if they shared the prejudices the old-timers had for half-breeds. Ellie hadn't said she'd been insulted or slighted in any way, but she was never one to complain about a thing like that anyway.

I didn't say anything until I finished eating, then I asked: "You working for any of the cowmen?"

"Breaking horses for the Circle A," he said.

He belched loudly and got up and left the house. He didn't say—"Good bye." "So long."—or anything. He just walked out. He'd left his saddle horse in the barn. A moment later we saw him ride into the street leading a loaded pack horse and turn west toward the Laramie range.

Ellie finished nursing the baby and handed him to me and buttoned her dress. I said: "Charley wasn't very talkative."

Ellie pulled her chair up to the table and began to eat. She shook her head at me as she asked: "Did you ever see him when he was?"

"No, but I've seen him when he could say longer sentences than he did tonight."

I looked down at Mick who was staring up at me as if he'd decided I was all right. I'd never been around babies, but he was fat and strong and happy, and he slept at least twenty hours out of the twenty-four. I figured we couldn't beat that.

"Charley likes Mick," Ellie said. "When he first saw him, he laughed more than I ever heard him laugh in his life and he said we sure are a couple of Sioux, meaning him and Mick."

"Mick will probably spend most of his time with Charley when he gets big enough," I said.

Ellie looked at me as if trying to read my mind. "What do you think now, Bill? About Mick?"

"He's a hell of a fine baby," I said. "Why?"

"I mean about looking like Charley."

"It doesn't bother me any," I said. "I figure it may make life hard for him when he gets bigger, though."

For a moment I thought she was going to cry, then she went on eating. Finally she said: "I know it will and I'm sorry. I tell him that every day, that I couldn't help it."

"Of course you couldn't, Ellie," I said. "Of course you couldn't."

It had never occurred to me she was blaming herself. It was stupid and I almost said so, then I knew it would be the wrong thing to say. She had never been one to blame anybody for anything and that included herself. Most of the time she was a very happy person, thankful for what life had brought to her. All I knew was that this was something she would have to work out for herself and there wasn't much I could do for her.

When she was done eating, she washed the dishes and put them away. By that time Mick was asleep. She lifted him out of my arms and laid him in his crib in the corner. When she turned back to me, I took her by the shoulder and pulled her to me and kissed her.

"Ellie, you don't know how good you've been for me or how much you've changed me," I said. "I don't understand it myself."

I told her about going out to the JM and Smoke Bunker's trying to kill me, and then I said: "What I hadn't really figured out before was that, if I hadn't hooked up with you, I would have ended up in a few years just like Bunker, a killer with a bullet in my brisket."

She tipped her head back and stared at me, wide-eyed, and then her lips began to quiver and she whispered: "Bill, you do belong to me, don't you?" She began to cry and she buried her face against my shirt. That was when I heard someone knock on the door.

I couldn't think of a worse time for anybody to come calling. It was probably Slim Galt and his wife Mirandy. Ellie ran to the stove and tried to regain control of herself. I walked to the door as I heard a second knock, and all the time I was searching my mind for some way to get rid of them.

I opened the door and there stood Jake Murdock. I forgot all about trying to get rid of our visitor. He was the last man on this green earth I expected to call on us. I just stood frozen, staring at him, and forgot the little I did know about manners.

Murdock asked: "Can I come in?"

I nodded and backed up, and he stepped into the room. Ellie had been wiping her eyes and sniffling, but I guess she recognized his voice because she turned as soon as she heard him.

I looked from Murdock to Ellie and back to Murdock, but I couldn't tell what either was thinking. I hoped, of course, that Ellie was happy with me and glad to be rid of Murdock, that Murdock was perfectly satisfied with Emily and his big spread.

After a long moment I was reasonably sure what was in Murdock's mind. He wasn't satisfied and he wished to hell he had Ellie back. It was as plain as Emily's dissatisfaction had been that afternoon.

"Howdy, Ellie," Murdock said.

She gave him a kind of curtsy and said gravely: "How are you, Jake?"

He glanced around the room, saw the crib, and walked to it. For what seemed a long time he stood looking down at the baby; then he turned and walked out, jerking his head at me as he passed me. I followed him to his horse, not having any idea what he wanted, but I was sure of one thing. I wasn't going to take any guff from him.

He stepped into the saddle and wiped a hand across his mustache.

I said: "Don't start taking my hide off because I didn't haul Ellie off to the reservation. She wouldn't go. Besides, I wanted her."

"Yeah," he said. "I knew that the first week you were cooped up in the house with her."

"No sense in you hating me because I've got her now," I said. "You had her and you threw her away."

"I don't hate you," he said.

"The hell you don't," I said. "You tried to get me killed today. Don't try it again."

"I didn't aim for it to work that way." He wiped his hand across his mustache again, then he asked: "Did you tell Emily about the baby?"

"No."

Still he sat there. In the starlight I couldn't see his face clearly, but I sensed he was having one hell of a fight inside to get said what he wanted to say. He blurted: "You going to raise the kid?"

"We'll raise him," I said. "I'll never tell him who his father is. I doubt that Ellie will, so if he's told, you'll be the one who tells him."

"It's better he don't know," he said gruffly, and rode away.

When I went back inside, Ellie asked: "Did you tell Jake this afternoon?"

"I told him," I said. "Nobody else heard."

"Not even his wife?"

"No."

"I hope Mick never knows," she said more to herself than to me. "I hope he never does."

I went to Rand's Bar that evening. Slim Galt was there along with Dr. Ross, Whipple, and several farmers. I said, loudly enough so they'd all hear: "I shot and killed Smoke Bunker this evening."

They heard me, all right. Rand stared at me, pop-eyed. The rest of them came to where I stood and wanted to know how it happened. I told them, and Rand slapped the bar with a palm of his fat hand and made the glasses jump.

"By God, I'm glad you done it," he said. "You just made yourself a reputation. I guess a man needs one if he's packing a star."

"We'll see," I said, and left the saloon.

He was right. That was the reason I told them, but I didn't think about it again on the way back to the house. I knew the story would soon get around. I thought about Ellie and Jake and me. I didn't hate him any more. He'd had his chance to keep Ellie and he'd thrown it away. I guess I really felt sorry for him, and I think he was envious of me.

Chapter Twenty-Five

It's kind of funny how a man can pack so much living into a few months or a year, then life levels out and he goes along for more months and years with nothing very exciting or important happening. Oh, you're getting a little older all the time. Babies are born. People die. Families move in. Other families move out. The pace of living slows down to a walk. I guess it's a case of living in the mountains for a time and then on a plateau.

Galt City did grow just as we expected. A brick factory was built on the edge of town. We soon had a dry goods store, several pool and billiard halls, a roller mill, a hardware store, several blacksmith shops, and a couple of livery stables, along with a tailor, barbers, lawyers, doctors, dentists, teachers, and the preachers for the three churches. Ellie went to the Methodist Church every Sunday morning and took Mick; she belonged to the Ladies' Aid, and, as far as I could tell, she liked it and felt accepted by the white women.

I don't know whether Whipple made anything on the lots he bought from me or not. During the summer a man named Dan Doyle came to town from Cheyenne, paid me $3,000 for my corner lot, put up a solid brick building, and started the Galt City State Bank.

When fall came, the boom had hit its peak and began to roll down the other side. Prices stabilized and by spring were down. I'm sure that some of the speculators who hung in there too long suffered a loss. I was glad I took Slim Galt's advice and sold out. I couldn't have hit it any better than I did.

The land on the flat was all taken and the reservoir and ditch system finished. The soil was rich for the most part and the farmers made money almost from the start. Clearing the land, of course, was not much of a problem.

We incorporated the town and Slim Galt was elected the first mayor. A few years later we organized Galt County and I was elected sheriff. Galt went back into the store and his son Jim took a job in my office as deputy. It was sort of understood that he'd be sheriff when I retired, but the joke was I had no immediate plans for retirement.

The cowmen all made money, especially Murdock who branched out into several lines of business. The biggest was supplying beef and hay and cordwood to Fort Laramie and Fort Fetterman. He was a busy man, on the go all the time.

Once in a while I'd see Emily in town and she'd admit she was pretty lonesome living in that big house by herself. She visited with the other ranchers' wives occasionally, but the big ranches were miles apart and she got so she just didn't have the energy to make the long drives.

I got along all right with Murdock after the night he dropped in on us. I'd run into him in Rand's Bar every month or so and buy him a drink or he'd buy me one and we'd talk. He'd ask about Ellie and about Mick, but he never came to the house again.

Sometimes he'd stand beside me at the bar and stare at his drink with a somber, distant expression on his face. I wondered if he was thinking of the old days when we'd been the best of friends and I'd ridden all over that corner of Wyoming with him slapping the JM iron on any unbranded calf we could find, or those hungry days when we'd been together on Crook's starvation march, wondering if we'd ever get our bellies full again.

We didn't hate each other now, but we didn't feel the same as we used to, either. He was rich and as arrogant as hell. The other ranchers looked to him for leadership and, without exception, did anything he wanted done, even to electing him to the state legislature.

He got over hating the town and the irrigation project. It was plain to everybody including Murdock that what had happened was to the cattlemen's advantage. Galt City was the closest place for them to trade. They could buy hay from the farmers for a more reasonable price than having it freighted up from Cheyenne. Aside from Doyle, the banker, and Slim Galt who came out of the boom with a fortune, the cowmen were the richest and most powerful men in the county, and nearly always we elected the county officials they selected.

Well, it wasn't that cut and dried, but that was what it amounted to.

Murdock took great delight in needling me about being sheriff. He'd say: "Bill, I think we need a new sheriff. You've had the job too long. I'm going to look around for a new man this fall."

I knew he was baiting me, but I'd get mad just the same. I'd say: "You go to hell. I don't have to risk my life packing a lousy star. I don't even have to live in Galt City."

Then he'd laugh like a fool and slap me on the back. "Kind o' thin-skinned, ain't you, son?"

The truth was he had become an unhappy man. He had every damned thing he had dreamed about, but it wasn't enough, now that he had it. I've often wondered what would have happened if he'd never met Emily. I think he would have shipped Ellie off to the reservation sooner or later and married a white woman, but he might have been happier than he was now because he wouldn't be seeing her or his son.

Emily stayed with him, although I think she was often tempted to leave him. She'd come to town once in a while and nurse for Dr. Ross, if he needed her, and I've got a hunch that this kept her sane more than anything else she did.

As for me, well, I couldn't have asked for a better life than I had. I just wouldn't have known what to ask for. I rode out across the flat almost every day, leaving Jim in the office in our fine new courthouse. Or I'd take all day and drop in on one of the ranches, have dinner with the rancher and his family, and ride back to town in the afternoon. In the evening, before I went to bed, I made the rounds of the saloons and whorehouses. The truth was we had about as little crime as a county could have.

Ellie? She was everything a woman should be to a man. I was thankful and I had enough sense to tell her so. I treated Mick as if he were my own son. Ellie and I had no children of our own, and I guess it was just as well, although Mick got along with the other kids and I never heard any of them calling him a "'breed" or "Injun" or "Sioux" or any other insulting name they might have used.

I bought a pinto pony for him and he started riding about the same time he learned to walk. Later I bought a bay mare for Ellie and the three of us would take Sunday afternoon rides in the summer or go camping and fishing, or sometimes just ride out to Charley Three Horses's ranch. The cowmen kept him busy breaking horses, but mostly he let people alone and they let him alone.

Mick was a good boy any way you looked at him. He did well in school, he minded either one of us, and he did his chores without any nagging. I don't think it ever occurred to him that he and Charley Three Horses were different from other people. Charley didn't tell him. Not then, anyway.

You live in Paradise for a while and you begin to think it's the natural way of life. I should have known better, of course. Man was born to trouble and the thunderheads had begun to appear along the horizon, but I wasn't looking for them.

First there was the tough winter of 1886–87, the so-called Big Die. We weren't hit the way the cattlemen were north of us, but we were hit hard enough. Somehow the Galt County stockmen staggered through, mostly because the bank stuck with them further and longer than they had a right to expect. Doyle could have closed most of them out, maybe all of them, and taken their ranches, but he didn't. Prices declined, too, which added insult to injury.

It didn't hurt me or the townspeople or the farmers except that we were naturally bound up together and business slacked off when the cowmen were hurt. Something else happened that spring which looked as if it were a blessing and in a way it was. The Cheyenne and Northern Railroad built north into Galt City.

The day the first train chugged into town, we had a hell of a big celebration: speeches, banners all over town, the band played, a barbecue, and dancing most of the night. Jim and I worked all night throwing drunks into jail and stopping fights and keeping an eye on everything in general.

When I went to bed at dawn, I thought it was great to have a railroad in Galt City. We could get to Cheyenne in two or three hours and connect with the Union Pacific and head east to Omaha or Kansas City or Chicago. Within a few months changes began taking place, subtle changes I couldn't really put my finger on, but changes I could feel.

Maybe it had been because we were more or less isolated that we had been a sort of big family, having some differences but still belonging to each other. Now we weren't isolated and people began going to Cheyenne or Denver just for the hell of it and strangers began coming to Galt City.

I ran several whores and a couple of gamblers out of town the first week. That didn't please some folks. I'll admit I was on shaky ground, but more whores and gamblers were the last people we needed.

I have no idea what brought it on, but now Mick began to realize he was different from other children. He played with them less and less, and he didn't want to do anything except live with Charley Three Horses. This pleased Charley but worried both me and Ellie. Presently Ellie dropped out of the Ladies' Aid and a few months later she quit going to church. She wouldn't tell me what happened, but I knew damned well something had been said or done to her.

"We can leave here," I told her. "I can resign as sheriff any time and Jim can fill in until next election."

"Oh, no," she said. "This is our home. We'll stay right here in Galt City."

I didn't know for sure what to do. I had invested most of my money in Cheyenne property and it was giving me a good return. We could move to Cheyenne or we could sell out and take our money and live anywhere we wanted to.

Later on, I wished we had done exactly that, but I'm not the seventh son of a seventh son, so I didn't know what we were heading into. Besides, I wasn't in the habit of forcing Ellie to do anything and she was adamant about staying in Galt City. I'm not sure why except that she had made up her mind a long time ago that she was not going to let her Indian blood change anything. It did change some things, of course, but they were conditions beyond her control.

For several years we got along. I mean Paradise had somehow eluded us. Not that we had any real trouble. Ellie had a few women friends she visited with. We rebuilt the house so we had the room we needed, something we had been intending to do for years but just hadn't taken the time and trouble and money to do.

Mick got into more fights than when he was smaller, but he was tough and strong and quick, so I didn't worry about him. He didn't want to move, mostly because he didn't want to leave his Uncle Charley.

The boy spent his vacations and weekends on Charley's horse ranch. We celebrated his sixteenth birthday in March, 1893. He was a tall, gangling boy who looked as if he had just sprouted up out of his boots. He was almost as brown-skinned as Charley, and almost as good with horses. He was a crack shot, both with a rifle and a revolver, and I couldn't keep from worrying about him because he turned sullen that summer and refused to go back to school in the fall. He stayed out there with Charley and that, of course, pleased Charley.

Then the panic hit us, and hell replaced Paradise.

Chapter Twenty-Six

Everyone in Galt County survived the panic. Oh, we were hurt, all right. No one is sacred in a period of national economic disaster, but we weren't hurt as much as the big industrial centers and mining camps were.

The bank didn't close, and I guess that was the key to what seemed to be a near miracle, but we congratulated ourselves too soon. By late winter and particularly early spring we realized we were not getting off scotfree.

Even before snow was off the ground, people began moving into Galt County and taking up homesteads. They came mostly in covered wagons pulled by skinny horses and held together by spit and baling wire, usually with a cow or two and a crate of chickens and a plow tied to the sides of the wagon.

They had children, hundreds of them it seemed, runny-nosed, thin-faced kids wearing clothes that had patches on top of patches. The women wore sunbonnets and faded calico dresses and must have been younger than they looked, and the men wore battered hats and run-over boots and pants as patched as their children's.

In general they were a poor lot—ignorant and lazy, the first to be fired from jobs if they'd had jobs before they showed up in Galt County, the first to get their credit cut off if they had a charge account at a store, and the first to expect a hand-out from those who survived the panic and were still in business.

I'm sure I'm exaggerating their faults, but I was like everyone else in Galt County. I was bitter about their coming. They reminded me of a plague of locusts. They came because we had free land where they could settle, never considering the fact that the land had been used by the big ranches as open range for years. They didn't give a second thought to what they could give to anyone else, but they sure gave a lot of thought to what they could get.

Some of them had a little money when they came; most of them were practically broke by the time they got to Galt County. A few of them rented houses in town and looked for jobs; most of them settled on the land wherever they could find water.

They started to plow the grass under, and, if they had money to buy barbed wire, they put up a fence around their quarter-section. The fact that dry farming wouldn't work here meant nothing to them. They said it hadn't been tried and kept right on plowing.

None of us welcomed the newcomers. All of us, farmers, townsmen, and ranchers agreed they were in the wrong place and doing the wrong thing. We let them know it plain out, but they weren't easily discouraged.

These people weren't at all like the settlers who had come during the boom days of the late 'Seventies. The latter had money to buy lots and build homes and start businesses in town, or take up land on the flat and pay for the water they needed and put up decent buildings. They'd been solid citizens, used to prosperity and willing to work hard to achieve it when they came to Galt County.

Most of the homesteaders who came now acted and looked as if they were beaten before they started. They were shifty-eyed and petulant, even quarrelsome. When Slim Galt and the other storekeepers refused credit, they were angry and said it was all a conspiracy to make them fail, that the cattlemen were to blame because they didn't want anyone plowing up the open range. They went to the bank and threatened Doyle when he turned them down.

The cowmen panicked and they had a right to. This kind of thing had happened in other parts of the cattle country, but I guess none of us had expected it to happen here. Murdock and the others tried to bluff these people off their homesteads, even to firing a few shots, but it didn't work. Of course, they came running to me for protection.

I didn't like the situation any better than the ranchers did. We'd had a balanced economy in Galt County, and I didn't want to see the boat rocked. I think Ellie and I had been happier before the railroad came to Galt City, maybe because Mick was small and needed us. He was a man now, or practically so, and he didn't need anybody unless it was Charley Three Horses.

Happiness, I suppose, is always a matter of degree. Life was good and had been right up to the invasion, as we called it. Now Jim Galt and I found ourselves in a position of having to defend these people against the cowmen and we both hated ourselves for it. For that matter, I guess the cowmen hated us, too.

Most of the homesteaders had time to plow a few acres and plant grain. We had a late snow, and, when it melted, the wheat came up, then we had a hot, dry spell, and by the end of June the wheat turned yellow. It was the sickest looking excuse for a crop I ever saw in my life.

If these people had had any sense, they would have realized they had done enough damage and moved on, but none of them would believe that this would happen every year. All they had to do was to hang on until next summer. This was an unusually dry season. You could tell them you had lived here almost twenty years and this was an average season, but they'd say you were lying to them because you wanted them to get out of the country.

I suppose this was the nearest to a home they had. Some had put up tar-paper shacks; others lived in tents or wagons. If they had arrived with a few dollars, it was gone now. They had nowhere else to go, and the ones I talked to didn't even have relatives they could live with until times improved and they could find jobs. A good many of the men had worked in the silver mines in Colorado and, of course, the silver market was not going to change with politics being what it was in this country.

I'll admit I got a little sick away down deep in my belly every time I visited any of these people. The babies were always crying. Not sick crying or mad crying, but hungry crying. The bigger kids were half-starved. The parents would ask me to stay for dinner, but I never did because I knew they didn't have anything to spare. I'd been around their places enough at mealtime to know what they had. It might be boiled wheat, or beans, and, if they had any meat, it probably was jack rabbit.

It seemed to me the churches should help the homesteaders. Not that I wanted them to stay. The county would be ruined if they did, and only their stupid stubbornness kept them hanging on. Still, I couldn't stand seeing the children go hungry day after day, so I'd take a side of bacon or a sack of flour to a family that was worse off than average.

Ellie often rode with me to see several families that had babies. Sometimes Emily Murdock would spend a day or more with one of them when the kids were sick, which usually just meant being half-starved.

No one in town approved of our doing anything for the homesteaders, and, if I suggested to the preachers or any of the church people that here was a case where charity should begin at home, I received an angry response to the effect that the homesteaders would be helped the minute they started moving on. More than that, I was told that Ellie and I were doing wrong if we took any food to them because we were encouraging them to stay.

Ellie and I soon learned that, if we did anything for these people, we had better do it on the sly. Public sentiment was one hundred percent against helping them, and I'll admit that any help I gave was against my better judgment.

What happened then was inevitable. I guess most honest men will turn dishonest if they are put under enough pressure, but I hadn't foreseen what was inevitable. Mick rode into town from Charley Three Horses's ranch one morning, early in July, and told me that one of Charley's prize young geldings had been stolen.

We'd never had any horse stealing in Galt County, so Charley naturally concluded that one of the homesteaders was the thief. They had tracked him for several miles, and, since he was going in the direction of Fort Laramie, they decided that was where he was taking the stolen horse. Charley sent Mick after me and he headed back to the ranch.

Mick rode to the fort with me. We didn't talk much. I hadn't seen anything of him all spring or early summer. We kept a room for him and some of his things were still there, but he hadn't slept in it for almost a year. Ellie was unhappy about it, but she didn't try to do anything or say anything to him.

One time, when I was talking to Ellie about Mick, she said sadly: "I gave birth to him, Bill. We raised him and we did the best we could for him. If he wants to live Charley's kind of a life, it's his privilege."

"Do you suppose he has any idea Jake is his father?" I asked.

"I don't know," she answered. "I've never told him, but maybe Charley has."

I had a hunch that was what had happened. Mick had changed from the time he was about ten or eleven, but it was only the last year or two that he'd turned sullen and had even quit calling me—"Pa"— which he had done all his life until then.

Charley was a loner and felt he had never been accepted by white people, and I wouldn't have put it past him to have told Mick just to turn him against us. I will say that Charley had always had a genuine affection for the boy, and I figured he would do about anything to get Mick to live with him.

Anyhow, Mick and I rode along side-by-side for the first time in months. He carried a .45 in a holster on his right hip and a .30-30 in the boot. He stared straight ahead, the same sullen expression on his dark face I had seen there ever since he'd gone to live with Charley. I hadn't seen him smile or heard him laugh for a long time.

He still had Murdock's square face and wide chin, but, with a skin as dark as his, I doubt that anybody figured out he was Murdock's son. Hardly anyone in the county knew of the relationship that had once existed between Ellie and Murdock nearly twenty years ago.

Just before we reached Fort Laramie, I asked: "You going into partnership with Charley someday?"

"No." He still didn't look at me, but continued to stare straight ahead. "I'll get hold of a thousand dollars someday, and, when I do, I'm getting to hell out of the country."

I had never heard as much bitterness in his voice as I heard just then, and I wondered about it. I wondered, too, how long it would take him to save $1,000. Charley was probably paying him thirty dollars a month and beans. I didn't ask him about it. I felt the way Ellie did. We'd done the best we could for him. From now on his life was up to him.

We found our man in Fort Laramie along with the stolen horse. Mick took the gelding back to the ranch and I took my prisoner to jail in Galt City. He was a young homesteader named Bud Call. When I asked him why he stole the horse, he said: "Sheriff, maybe you've never been hungry, real hungry. If you had been, you'd know."

When I got back to the courthouse, Jim Galt was waiting for me. He said bluntly: "We're in for it, Bill. The homesteaders are stealing beef."

I sat down at my desk and filled my pipe. I thought about it and decided it was to be expected. I asked: "To eat?"

He nodded. "It's been going on for several weeks, or so the cattlemen claim. A committee came to see you today, Chick Bromley and Jake Murdock and Dan Gibson. Bromley done the talking. They want you to come to an association meeting at the JM at eight o'clock tomorrow night. They wouldn't tell me what they planned, but it don't look good."

"I guess I'd better be there," I said.

I thought about it all the way home. I was tempted to resign and let Jim take the sheriff's job. Mick didn't need Ellie and me any more and I didn't have to have the sheriff's salary. To hell with it. Ellie and I could live the rest of our lives on what we had. We could go somewhere else and buy a small spread and not have a care in the world.

But I didn't resign. I guess I knew all the time I wouldn't.

Chapter Twenty-Seven

I had never attended a meeting of the Galt County Cattlemen's Association. I had no right to go, not being a member, and I had never been invited. I didn't know why I had been invited tonight, but I soon found out after I got to the JM.

They were all there ahead of me, fifteen of them crammed into Murdock's front room. I suppose they had talked their business over before I got there. Anyhow, Murdock met me outside as I dismounted and said: "Bill, don't lose your temper tonight."

I didn't know what he meant. I didn't have a hair-trigger temper, and he knew it. I looked at him as we walked up the path to the front door. I couldn't see him well enough in the thin light to make out his expression. I asked: "What's up?"

"You'll find out," he said.

I knew that was all I'd get out of him then, so I didn't press the matter, but I had the impression he didn't like any part of it. I followed him into the house, nodded as some of them said—"Howdy, Sheriff"—and sat down near the door.

I didn't know how they were organized, but I had supposed Murdock was a sort of perpetual president of the outfit. As far as I knew, he had pretty well dictated policy from the time it had been organized fifteen years before.

I soon saw I was wrong about Murdock. At least he wasn't chairing this meeting. Chick Bromley got up and worked his way through the crowd to the fireplace. He stood with his back to it and looked at us for a few seconds. Not at me particularly. Just at all the men in front of him.

"The meeting will come to order," Bromley said finally. "This will be an informal session. We will not keep minutes because we don't want any record of what we say tonight. More than that, when we walk out of this house, we will forget what has been said."

I had a funny feeling when he started talking. By the time he finished, the feeling was more than funny. It was downright weird. I had never felt that way before in my life. I don't think I was scared. Still, it was hard to tell just what the feeling was. For one thing, the men in the room stopped talking, they stopped smoking, they even stopped moving. For a time I thought they had stopped breathing.

For one thing I had a different notion about Chick Bromley than I'd ever had before. He was a small man in his middle thirties, five feet six or seven inches with a black mustache and black brows and thin, cruel lips. He was as evil as hell. I sensed that as surely as I sensed that he had these men under his thumb and that included Jake Murdock. This was queer in itself. Most of these men had big out-fits, but Bromley just had a shirt-tail spread over on Sybille Creek. I didn't know much about him except that he was a proddy son-of-a-bitch, but I'd heard talk that he was a killer and had had to leave Texas in a hurry. I suddenly believed everything I had heard about the man.

He must have been silent and motionless for a full minute. I could hear some of the men breathing; I could hear a clock on the mantle behind Bromley going *tick-tock, tick-tock.* The ticking seemed to boom into the silence, sounding louder than any clock I'd ever heard before. I looked at the clock. It was then seven minutes after eight.

"We're all in the same boat," Bromley resumed. "When the sodbusters started moving into Galt County last March, we tried to run a bluff on 'em. It didn't work, partly because we weren't hurting yet and we didn't make it stick, but mostly because our sheriff let us know these bastards would get the pro-tection of the law."

He looked right at me. There wasn't any doubt about it. His gaze was pinned squarely on me. For the first time I realized he hated me with a deep and passionate hatred that went far beyond the limits of reason. Maybe it was because I wore a star. Some men who have been on the run feel that way toward any and all lawmen.

He was silent, letting the tension build until I thought I couldn't stand it another second, then he went on in a cold, ugly voice: "We have paid the sheriff's salary with our taxes for years. These peo-ple he's been protecting have paid nothing. They have done nothing except destroy what we have spent a generation building. Now they are stealing our cattle, butchering them, and living off them right under our noses, and the sheriff does nothing."

I'd been taken by surprise. I was shocked, I guess, but I hadn't come here to take a currying like this. I jumped up, calling: "Now hold on, Bromley . . . !"

A couple of big hands grabbed me from behind and jammed me back into my seat. Dan Gibson who owned Wineglass on the Platte north of town said: "Let him finish, Lang."

I waited until he let go, then I slid sideways out of my chair and got my back to the wall. I had my gun in my hand when I faced him. I said: "Gibson, you put a hand on me like that again and I'll blow your ugly snoot right out through the back of your head."

If anyone had dropped a pin at that moment, it would have sounded like a railroad spike in the room. Murdock said: "Better let Bromley finish, Bill."

I turned my head to look at Bromley. I said: "You boys ought to know . . . and I think you do . . . that I don't like these homesteaders moving in any more than you do, but that doesn't change the law. Whoever pays my salary with his taxes can't change the law to suit himself, either. Now, if you brought me here to argue about . . ."

"No," Bromley said. "We brought you out here to tell you we aim to get these people out of Galt County before it's too late. We'll tell you how we propose to do it. All we want from you now is a promise to go fishing. Tonight."

It struck me how little this kind of thing had changed in almost twenty years. Here was Chick Bromley talking for the cattlemen of Galt County.

He figured they were above the law, as arrogant as the big cow outfits had been that I'd worked for as a young man. The difference was that in those days I was a hired killer. Now that I was on the other side of the fence, they were telling me to go fishing.

"No," I said. "I'm afraid I can't do that."

"Then you'll be sorry," Bromley said coldly, "and you'll wish you had. When the next election comes around, we'll pick a different man. If we had known at the last election what we know about you now, you wouldn't be carrying that star."

"To hell with you," I said. "I don't have to have the job."

I swung toward the door, then stopped when Murdock called: "Wait, Bill! I think you'd better hear this."

I looked at him. His face had turned brick red. More than ever I thought he didn't like any part of what they were planning, but he'd been outnumbered and outvoted, and he probably figured he had to go along. Still, I wasn't prepared for what they were planning when I looked at Bromley and said: "Well?"

"They've all been warned today to be on the road out of Galt County by tonight," Bromley said in that same cold, ugly tone he had been using. "As far as I know, none of them has started, so they need a push. The situation has reached the place where the only solution is a funeral or two. We've decided that an exterminator can do the job quick and sudden, so we've thrown one thousand dollars into the pot to hire one."

I was so angry that it took me several seconds to grasp fully what he had just said, and, when I did, I still couldn't believe it. I said: "My God, you're talking about murder. You can't mean it."

"We mean it," Bromley said.

He meant it, all right. I looked at him, and then at Murdock. I said: "Jake, are you standing still for this?"

"It's the way we voted," he said thickly. "I don't have no choice."

"That's right," Gibson said. "The vote was fourteen to one. He was the one. You've had plenty of time to get these bastards off our range and out of the county, Lang. You didn't do it, so we'll take whatever steps we have to."

"We've waited too long now," Bromley said. "We won't sit on our butts and lose everything we've got."

"If you go ahead with this," I said, "you'll all be guilty of murder."

"You try arresting one of us," Bromley said, "just any of us, and you'll be in more trouble than you ever dreamed about. We'll swear you're lying and that everything you've just heard wasn't said here tonight. Not a word of it. And if you're stupid enough to bring one of us to trial, you'll never get a jury in this county to convict us."

I wheeled to the door and walked out, knowing he was right. I mounted and rode back to town, feeling that I'd just had a nightmare and I'd wake up and find I'd been asleep. When I got back to Galt City and put my horse up, I found Jim Galt in the courthouse, waiting to hear what had happened. I told him and he sat on the other side of the desk and didn't move. By that time I knew this was no nightmare.

When I finished, I asked: "Suppose I resign? What would you do?"

"Just what you'll do," he said. "I'm no hero, but I respect the law. It wasn't made to suit those fifteen men." Then he shrugged. "But, hell, you're not going to resign. I know you too well. Not now when this is hanging fire anyway."

"No," I said. "I guess not."

I filled my pipe and lit it, and we sat there in silence a long time, smoking and thinking, and not knowing quite what to do. I hadn't fully realized how much I'd changed since I'd killed a man on the Picketwire in southern Colorado for no better reason than that was what I'd been hired to do.

But I had changed, and somehow I had to make up for that killing. I couldn't bring the poor devil back to life. All I could hope to do was to keep some other men from being killed who were in the same position the man on the Picketwire had been. Right now I didn't know how to do that.

At length I said: "I'm going home and going to bed." Jim nodded. "So am I."

Once I did go to sleep, I had a wild dream that I was riding hell for leather on Sundown, trying to get away from the Sioux. Sundown had died four years ago and I felt as if I had lost a member of the family. Since then I'd been riding a horse I'd bought from Charley I called Diablo because he was as black as the devil. He was a good horse and I liked him. Of course, he wasn't what Sundown had been, but then I'd never find another horse like Sundown.

The Sioux didn't have a chance of catching Sundown, and I was putting more daylight between us all the time when Ellie shook me awake. "Bill, wake up," she said, "Wake up. There's someone at the door."

I pulled on my pants and lit the lamp, thinking that some of that crazy bunch of murdering cowmen were getting me out of bed trying to make me go fishing. I put the lamp down on the stand in the front room and opened the door. Jake Murdock was standing there. It wasn't full daylight, but there was enough light to see he was about as pale as I had ever seen him.

"Come outside," he said. "Shut the door."

I stepped onto the porch and shut the door. When you've been in tough situations as much as I have, you get so you sense when a man is scared, scared so much it reaches all the way down into the bottom of his guts. I think there must be a peculiar smell you catch without really knowing it's a smell. You hear about dogs and horses sensing when a man's scared, and I always figured they caught the fear smell. Anyhow, I knew this about Murdock as soon as I stepped outside.

I stood there, looking at him for several seconds while the corners of his mouth worked, and it took that long before he could control himself enough to say: "Bill, they've hired Mick to murder the Newton brothers."

I backed up against the door and leaned there. I couldn't breathe for a time and my heart was hammering so hard it was about to jump out of my throat and my knees turned to water. Now I was the one who couldn't say anything. I don't know what I expected to happen, but it certainly wasn't this.

Then I remembered Mick's saying that he was going to get his hands on $1,000 and get to hell out of the country. Last night Bromley had said that the association had $1,000 in the kitty to hire an exterminator.

Murdock had his voice then. He hurried on: "I fought it as hard as I could. I said we'd wind up getting martial law for Galt County and all of us would go to jail for murder, but I couldn't stop 'em. I guess some of 'em, Gibson and Bromley anyway, had already talked to Mick and made their proposition, and he'd told them he'd take it. So after you left, Gibson rode to the horse ranch to get Mick."

"When is he supposed to rub them out?" I asked.

"Now," he answered. "This morning. He's to shoot 'em down when they leave their shack to go to the shed to milk."

Now! The word was like a fist hitting me in the belly. I figured there wasn't time to stop him because the Newtons would be getting up before long, but we had to try. I said: "Go get Jim. Meet me at the Newton place."

I ran back inside and went into the bedroom and dressed as fast as I could. Ellie asked: "What's going on? Who was it?"

"Jake." I couldn't tell her what was going on, so I lied to her. "That fool cattlemen's association is fixing to rub out some of the homesteaders. We'll stop them if we can."

Well, it wasn't really a lie. It just wasn't the whole truth. If Mick did this and I had to arrest him, I didn't know what it would do to Ellie. If he ended up getting hanged for it . . .

I couldn't think that far ahead. Ellie never said much about Mick any more. We could rationalize about it until we were black in the face and say we'd done all we could for Mick. We'd given him a good home and we'd loved him and we hadn't spoiled him, but the fact remained that Ellie was part Indian and Mick, who was her son, had by an accident of birth inherited a brown skin that set him apart from the other boys in the county and had turned his thoughts inward so that he had, in effect, run away to his uncle's horse ranch. Maybe it wasn't true that he was an outcast, but I'm sure he felt cut off from doing the things that boys of his age could do.

No, Ellie wasn't to blame, and yet she was to blame in the sense that, if Mick had had an all-white mother, he would have had a white skin and he would have been like everybody else. So, if he killed these men, she could blame herself, even though she could honestly say she had done all she could for him.

I grabbed my gun belt and ran out of the house, worrying about Ellie a good deal more than about Mick. I saddled Diablo and headed west toward the Newton homestead on the dead run. One of the Newton brothers was in his early twenties, the other was a teen-ager a little older than Mick. They were among the best of the newcomers, having had a little money and a number of Jersey cows that they milked.

Once a week they brought the cream into town, and so had a small cash income that was enough to buy their grub. It was irony, I thought, that the cattlemen would pick these two for murder, the least likely of all the homesteaders to steal and butcher any range cattle.

The Newton shack was in the bottom of a draw. When I reached the ridge crest above it, I was shocked to see half a dozen men milling around between the shack and the slab shed. I roared down the slope, and, when I got closer, I saw that Mick was there and that the Newton boys were on the ground, dead.

I pulled up and hit the ground running. The men were all homesteaders. They had seen me coming, all right, but it hadn't made any difference to them. They had Mick and were roughing him up and cursing him and saying he'd better admit he'd done it. His nose was bleeding and the left corner of his mouth was cut and one eye was black.

I yanked my gun out of leather and I sailed into them, swinging the gun barrel like a club. I knocked one man down and put another one on his knees, and about that time the rest backed off and let me have Mick.

"What's this about?" I demanded. "I've got a notion to jail the bunch of you for assault and battery."

"Sure, you damned Cossack!" one of them yelled. "The cattlemen own you, don't they?"

Another one said: "He's your kid. I guess he could murder a couple of us and you wouldn't touch him."

I didn't know the first one, but the second man was Luke Perkins, the nearest neighbor the Newton boys had. He was a big man, shaggy and dirty and smelly. He had a slattern for a wife and ten kids. Or eleven. I wasn't sure, although Ellie would know because she'd brought stuff out here for their babies. To me he was typical of the worst of the homesteaders.

I was sore, sore enough that I didn't care much what I said or did. He wasn't wearing a gun, but if he'd had one, I might have hoorawed him into pulling it so I could have killed him. That was the way I felt, anyhow, and it struck me that, if Bromley and Gibson and the rest of the cattlemen had any sense, they'd have had Perkins rubbed out, not the Newton brothers. The chances were good that Perkins had been stealing and butchering range cattle. I don't know how else his brood of kids could have lived the last three or four months if he hadn't.

It took me a while to control my tongue. When I could, I said: "Perkins, you open your mug again while I'm here and I'll take my gun barrel and knock your teeth down your throat." I looked around at the rest. "If one of you has a decent tongue in his head, tell me what happened."

A man named Stell, who lived about half a mile to the north, said: "I'll tell you, Sheriff." He glanced around at the others, then moved so his back was to the dead men. "We heard some shooting a little while ago. We'd agreed to meet at Perkins's place before sunup. We were fixing to go hunting, figuring we could bring back meat for all of us. We headed here as soon as we heard the shooting and found him"—he jerked a thumb at Mick—"bending over the dead men. His rifle had been fired recent, so we figured he was the one who done it, all right. We was trying to get a confession out of him when you rode up."

After hearing what Murdock had told me a few minutes ago, I had a notion they were right, but I wasn't going to tell them what Murdock had said, and I doubted that Murdock or any of the other cowmen would say anything about Mick's being hired by them. Just then Murdock and Jim Galt broke over the crest of the ridge and came thundering down the slope.

"I'll take Mick to jail," I said. "You men clear out."

"We'll take the bodies," one of the men said. "They were our friends."

I shook my head. "I'll take them to town. The coroner will want to look at them before he makes a report. You can get the bodies when he's done with them."

Still they hesitated, looking at each other uneasily, then at me. Then one said: "We'll tell you something, Sheriff. We were all warned to leave the country. We didn't go, so it looks purty plain that these two killings are aimed at making up our minds for us. Well, you can tell your cattlemen friends we ain't going. If you all don't hang this lad for murder, we will."

They mounted and rode away just as Murdock and Jim reined up and dismounted. Murdock and I exchanged glances. I guess both of us were thinking I'd been too late to save the Newton boys' lives. It just never occurred to me that Mick hadn't done the killing. I didn't say anything about what Murdock had told me in front of Jim. I didn't know what Murdock had told him, and I sure didn't want to say anything that might be mentioned under oath at the trial that might work against Mick.

I studied the boy's face for a moment. There were times when I thought I knew him, but at other times—and right now was one of them—I felt as if he were a complete stranger who had shut me completely out of his life.

"Did you do it, Mick?" I asked.

"I got nothing to say," he answered.

He had a sullen set to his mouth that told me he wasn't going to tell me a thing. I didn't ask him anything else. I saw him look briefly at Murdock, and then turn his back to him. I figured right then that he knew who his father was. Charley Three Horses had told him, and now he hated both of us.

I went to where Jim was kneeling beside the dead men. They lay about ten feet from the door of their shack. Both had been shot in the chest and probably had been killed immediately. Milk buckets were on the ground beside the bodies. I went inside and looked around, but I didn't see anything that told me more than I knew.

"Looks to me like the god-damned cowmen hired the boy," Jim said in a low tone. "They're the ones who ought to hang."

"Yeah, they're the ones," I said.

We pulled the door shut and went to the shed and harnessed the horses and hooked them up to the wagon. We lifted the bodies into the bed and covered them with blankets from the bed in the house. I asked Jake to drive the wagon to town and he nodded.

"Mount up," I said to Mick.

We rode back to Galt City, the boy between me and Jim. None of us said a word until we reached the courthouse and went in. We searched Mick. Besides the usual odds and ends such as a pocket knife, some fishhooks, and a handful of copper rivets, we found one hundred dollars in greenbacks.

When we locked Mick in a cell, I asked: "Do you want to say anything now?"

"No."

That was all. One word, one syllable, and judging from the stubborn, set expression on his face, that was all he was going to say.

Chapter Twenty-Eight

Mick was tried early in October. During all those weeks from the time I had arrested him until he walked into the courtroom I had not been able to get a statement of any kind from him. He wouldn't even tell me how he'd got the one hundred dollars we'd found on him the day we'd brought him in.

Jim Galt couldn't do any better. Neither could Ellie who visited Mick every day and brought him little tidbits to eat. He did finally tell her he didn't kill the Newton brothers. Beyond that he would say nothing.

The best lawyer in town was John Pryor and Pryor was hired to defend Mick. It was a badly kept secret that the cattlemen's association was paying Pryor, although no one said it openly, and I'm sure it could not have been proved. The lawyer spent a lot of time with Mick, but I never did find out how much of a statement Mick made to him.

Charley Three Horses always came to see the boy

when he was in town. He wouldn't tell me much, either, except when I asked him if he knew where Mick got the one hundred dollars, he said: "Hell, no."

"Was it wages you paid him?" I asked.

Charley grinned. "He buried his wages. It's still buried." Then the grin died and he added sourly: "He'll vamoose when he gets out of jail."

The more I thought about it, the more certain I was that Mick didn't kill the Newton brothers. The only thing that made him look bad was the fact he just wouldn't talk. If he would tell where he had been all night and why he was there at the Newton place and explain why his rifle had been fired, I had a notion he'd get off scotfree. If he didn't talk, he might swing. I guess I worried as much as Ellie did.

Murdock had very little to say about the whole business. I heard he had quit going to the association meetings, so I figured he was sore at all of them. I don't think he was against the proposition of rubbing out a few homesteaders, but I did think he had tried to keep them from hiring Mick.

One day I ran into him in Rand's Bar and asked him who he thought had done the killing. He just shook his head. "I dunno. After you left the JM that night, we almost had a fight. We argued about it till just before I got you out of bed, though Bromley had got sore and left a long time before that. Gibson was gone, too. By the time we broke up, they was so mad at me they wouldn't tell me nothing. I guess they'd actually made the deal with Mick before I knew anything about it. Maybe what they did tell me wasn't the exact truth."

"Bromley might have done the killing," I said.

"Mick had one hundred dollars on him, but Bromley might have kept the other nine hundred, if he was the one who done the collecting."

Murdock nodded. "It was Bromley, and that was just about the way I think it happened, but how can you prove it?"

You couldn't, of course, especially since Mick wouldn't talk. I had a hunch he was keeping his mouth shut, thinking the association would pay him for that. I told him he was crazy, that he was risking his neck for nothing, and he'd never get another penny, but he just stared at me, his lips pulled tight, his dark eyes expressionless.

A few of the homesteaders had packed up and left the county. Jim and I had arrested a couple of them for butchering range cattle, but we both did a lot of riding and we found mighty little evidence of stealing. I don't think there had ever been much, and I believe Bromley had built the butchering business out of proportion to get the other cowmen worked up. That hadn't been hard, with all of them hating the homesteaders the way they did because their range was being plowed up. Maybe it was just an excuse for all of them so they could hire a killer with a free conscience.

Most of the homesteaders were still hanging on. It seemed to me they were staying just to see Mick hang for murder. Not a day passed but what I'd see a bunch of them in town, more often than not just standing on the street in little knots, all of them armed, all of them hating me and Jim and the townsmen and the cattlemen and Mick most of all. At least one or more would tell me every day including Sunday that Mick would never leave Galt City if he was acquitted.

On the day the trial started there must have been fifty of them in town. Just the men. They'd left their women and children at home. They wandered up and down Main Street, aimlessly it appeared, but I had a notion it wasn't aimless at all. I think they wanted to be seen.

A few carried pistols, but most of them had shotguns or rifles, generally old models, but they'd work well enough to kill a man. There was no laughter among the homesteaders, not much talk, and they notified every businessman on Main Street that if Mick was acquitted, they would burn the town.

I was in the courthouse all morning, not leaving until noon when I went to the hotel for dinner. That was when I heard the burning threats. The townsmen would make up the jury along with farmers from the irrigation project, and I suppose the talk was aimed at intimidating them. As soon as I had a few names of the men making the threats, I arrested them one at a time for disturbing the peace and jailed them. By the middle of the afternoon the rest had gone home.

Murdock was the only cowman in town except the few who were on the jury panel. I asked him if he thought any of them would give Jim and me some help if we needed it and he said no. They didn't want to get involved. They didn't even want it to get out that they were paying Mick's lawyer, and naturally they didn't want the public to know they had planned to murder a couple of homesteaders, so the safest thing to do was simply to stay home and keep out of the whole affair.

By evening the jury had been picked, five towns-men and seven farmers. The others on the panel were dismissed. This included three ranchers who got out of town as soon as they could saddle their horses.

I didn't expect any trouble that night with the homesteaders. Still, there was always the danger of a lynch party in a situation like this, and that was the one thing I would never allow to happen, so Jim and I set up cots in the courthouse. Murdock spent the first part of the night in Rand's Bar until it closed, then he came to the courthouse.

Murdock didn't say much at first. Sure, I knew the old days were gone forever and you don't roll back eighteen years as if they had never been. Still, it was a comfort to have him there, and whatever hate I'd felt for him at one time was gone. We hadn't really talked since I left Crook City. I sent Jim to the hotel for coffee, then I told him to go home, that he'd sleep better in bed with his wife and he said he guessed he would.

After he left, Murdock and I sat up in the office drinking coffee, not talking, but both thinking, I guess, of the good days long gone.

I tipped back my chair and looked at him. He was pushing fifty, a graying giant of a man, as strong as he ever was, but somehow seeming to fade these last months. He had a lot of lines in his face, and his great, sweeping mustache had turned almost white. I had the notion he was burned out, that the old drive was gone and he was just a shell of the Jake Murdock I had ridden with eighteen years ago.

"Funny thing," he said suddenly. "By God, you turned out to be the solid one, Bill. I seen you as just a drifting gunfighter I could maybe talk into staying with me. I knew I could use you. You were beholden to me for saving your life, and I figured I'd take advantage of that. You didn't seem to want anything, and I wanted the world. I could see that Ellie struck your fancy. I didn't care if you got in bed with her when I was gone all day. I was aiming to ship her off to the reservation anyway. But you wound up owning the world, and I wound up with the taste of ashes in my mouth. How did it happen, Bill?"

I filled my pipe and looked at him, and then I understood. He was a dissatisfied, empty man, even more than I had thought.

"I don't know, Jake," I said, "but you've got Emily and you've got the JM, the biggest spread in this corner of the state. You've been to the legislature. You've hobnobbed with the big guns in the capital. You even went back to Washington once. I'm just the sheriff of Galt County."

He was dribbling tobacco into his pipe. Now he stopped and looked at me and I thought he was going to cry. He said: "Yeah, that's what I've done. I've got to where I wanted to go, only now that I've got there, it ain't where I want to be. You see, I was blind. Ellie loved me and I didn't know what that meant. I just didn't know what it meant to live all this time without being loved by nobody." He choked up for a moment, then he tamped the tobacco down into the bowl of his pipe. He said, staring at the pipe in his hand: "Emily and me never made no pretense of loving each other. She was never worth a damn in bed. She had money and she let me have it and she never let me forget it. We made a deal. I wanted a big ranch. She wanted a husband. Don't ask me why. I think it was because she had a holy terror of being an old maid, but there never has been a day since then when I didn't wish I had Ellie back and Emily didn't wish she had her money in the bank."

I fired my pipe and wondered what I could say to that. I had no regrets about my life except a wish that I could have done better raising Mick, but Ellie and I had done the best we knew how, so there was no real reason for regrets.

"It would have helped if Emily and me had had some kids," Murdock went on, "but we didn't and we won't." He jerked his thumb toward the cells. "I can't even claim the one boy I have sired. I can't even tell him I'm his father. I don't care if he has got a brown skin. By God, he's my son. You're gonna need my help before this is over. You won't get no help from the farmers or the townspeople, and the ranchers don't want to get their necks in a wringer. I figure it's up to me and you and Jim Galt."

"I'd appreciate your help," I said.

We went to bed after that, but we didn't sleep much. We had our guns on the floor beside our heads so we could put our hands on them in a hurry, and we kept our pants on. We stayed awake listening for the sound of men breaking into the courthouse, but daylight came finally and nothing had happened.

Murdock sat up and swung his feet to the floor. He seemed old and gaunt and gray. Suddenly I was shocked by a weird feeling that came to me as I stared at him in the thin light. The look of death was on him.

Chapter Twenty-Nine

That morning the homesteaders were back in town, tight-lipped, truculent, and proddy. I didn't count them, but there must have been fifty or sixty of them. More rode into town during the morning, so by noon there must have been seventy of them.

It was a strange thing, I thought. By spring, when it was time to plant crops, there wouldn't be ten of them left in the country, but they were determined to stay long enough to hang the boy they believed had murdered two of them. After that, they'd drift away.

A few of them, the neighbors like Perkins and Stell, were called as witnesses. They told with considerable relish how they had gathered at Perkins's place, had heard two shots, and had gone immediately to the Newton homestead and had caught Mick bending over their bodies.

The boy's rifle had unquestionably been fired recently, or so they all thought. Two empty .30-30 shells were on the ground a few feet from the bodies. They all swore they had been ordered by the cowmen to leave the county and they knew the Newton brothers had received the same warning.

Pryor did a good job cross-examining them. Before he got done, he made them all do a good deal of squirming. He forced them to admit they had not seen Mick do the shooting, that the Newton brothers were dead when they arrived, and they could not say from their own observation and knowledge that Mick had killed them.

I had to testify later in the day about what I had seen when I got there. Jim Galt was called, and finally Murdock. I don't think our testimony was damaging, although Jim and I had to tell about the one hundred dollars we had found on Mick. It struck me that the state had a pretty weak case. I just couldn't believe that a man would be hung for murder because he was found bending over two murdered men.

When I left the courthouse to meet Ellie for supper in the hotel dining room, Perkins and Stell and several other homesteaders were waiting for me in front of the courthouse. Perkins said: "We'd better not get a miscarriage of justice. If that jury knows what's good for it, it'll find the kid guilty. He's going to hang whether they do it or not."

"You won't hang him," I said.

"There'll be a hundred of us in town tomorrow morning just waiting to hear the jury's verdict," Perkins said. "You think your cattlemen friends that hired the kid will give you a hand?"

"No," I said. "It'll just be me and my deputy. If Mick is found not guilty, Jim Galt and I will take him out of the courthouse and put him on his horse and send him back to the ranch where he works. You won't lay a hand on him."

"Two of you against a hundred of us?" Perkins shook his head as if he could not understand my stupidity. "You must think you're both ten feet tall."

"We are," I said.

I walked past him toward the hotel. You never know about men. Take these homesteaders one at a time and they weren't much. Ignorant, dirty, shiftless, a no-good lot looking for something for nothing, generally speaking. But you put them together in a mob and you have something else. They lose their identity and they unite into some kind of a horrible, deadly monster.

By the time I reached the hotel, I was a little jumpy. Ellie noticed it at once and put her hand on my arm. She asked: "What is it?"

"The homesteaders figure they're going to lynch Mick if he's found not guilty," I said. "Jim and me can handle them, if they try anything, but some of them might get drunk tonight and come to the house. I'm going to stay at the jail again tonight, so I want you to sleep here in the hotel."

"I'm not afraid," she said.

"I know you're not," I said, "but I am."

She smiled then and shook her head. "Don't try to fool me. I know you too well. You're not afraid of anything."

"You're dead wrong about that," I told her. "I'm afraid of something happening to you. I know what men like this can do. If they decide they might not be able to get at Mick, they'll take it out on his mother."

"All right," she said. "I'll stay here." She didn't

say anything more until we sat down at a table, then she leaned forward: "Bill, get help from somebody. You and Jim can't fight off a mob like that. Won't the association help you?"

"I wouldn't ask them," I said. "It's up to the sheriffs office to handle law and order in the county. I doubt that they'd do anything if I did ask. They're paying for Mick's lawyer, and that's about as deep as they're going to get into it."

"Charley would help you, if you ask him," she said.

I knew what it would do to a half-breed to get involved in a deal like this, but I didn't say that to Ellie. "He's getting along all right," I said. "Let's leave it that way."

"What about Jim's dad?" she asked. "He'd help. There must be others here in town who'd help if they were asked."

"Slim's an old man now," I said impatiently. "I won't ask any of them for help. They're paying me and Jim good salaries to handle situations like this. We're supposed to be fighting men. They're not."

"But against odds like that," she said. "Nobody has the right to ask that even of fighting men."

"I've faced odds before," I said. "I can do it again." The waitress came and took our order. When she left, I said: "Looks to me as if you don't think Jim and I can handle this."

"Oh, Bill, I know you can." She smiled and leaned forward and covered my hand that was on the table with hers. "It's just that I'm afraid for you. I wouldn't want to live if anything happened to you. You're a strong, hard man when you have to be, but you're not afraid to show that you love me, too."

I looked down at my plate for a while. She got to

me when she said that. I thought of Murdock and how much our lives would have been different if he had realized that love was an important part of a man's life. But he hadn't and now he had only regrets. I didn't tell her what he had said. I didn't think it was the right time.

When we finished eating, I walked home with her. She filled a small valise with what she would need for the night and I walked back to the hotel with her. Perkins and Stell and several other homesteaders stood on the boardwalk along Main Street, watching us.

Their hate was more than a feeling. I suppose they were the kind of men who hated anyone with authority and they certainly hated men who had wealth such as a banker or a cattleman, but whatever the cause of it was, it seemed to me that their hate was a tangible force that reached out and touched me as I walked past them.

I thought again how they were cowards as individuals, but put them together and they became a murdering mob. If I'd had any doubt about there being trouble tomorrow, it was gone now. Trouble was as inevitable as the sunrise.

I left Ellie in her room and returned to the courthouse. I kept Jim with me until Murdock came, then I told him to make the rounds of the saloons and brothels around midnight to see if the homesteaders were up to anything.

I felt something was wrong with Murdock when he first came in, but I didn't ask and he didn't tell me until Jim left, then he said gravely: "I sure as hell did the wrong thing. I sent several of my crew after Bromley. I guess I should have told you what I was figgering on, but it didn't seem like it could go wrong. It did, though. Bromley said to hell with 'em and made a fight out of it. They killed him."

"Then I guess we'll never get the truth out of him," I said.

I was sore, Murdock's jumping the gun that way and not saying anything about it. I'd been thinking right along that Mick hadn't shot the Newton brothers, and, when the trial was over, that I'd ride out to Bromley's ranch and get the truth out of him. Now we would never know for sure.

"The jury will acquit the boy," Murdock said. "They're gonna have to. Hell, they don't have no case against him."

"Only there'll be a hundred homesteaders out in front, waiting with a rope, the minute he's a free man," I said.

"We'll handle 'em," Murdock said. "He'll ride out of town and be a free man. You'll see." He hesitated, scratching his stubble-covered chin, his gaze on something that was far away. "I wish the boy could have known that I . . ." Then he shrugged. "Hell, it's too late now. I can think of a dozen things I should have done, but it's too late for any of 'em."

We slept a little better that night, but not much. In the morning I brought Mick's breakfast, then went back to the hotel and ate with Ellie. I asked: "You coming to the trial this morning? I understand that Pryor's going to put Mick on the stand and that's about all the defense he'll make. I guess he thinks he raised enough doubt in the jury's mind yesterday in his cross-examination."

"I'll be there," she said.

"You stay inside the courthouse till the trouble's

over," I said. "I don't want the homesteaders grabbing you for a hostage."

"All right." She looked at me, her eyes grave. "You said trouble?"

"That's exactly what I said," I told her. "But don't worry, we'll handle it."

"Don't worry," she mimicked. "Of course I won't worry. Not one little bit."

I didn't say anything, but I didn't feel like making a joke out of it.

Pryor finished the defense in a hurry, just as I'd said. He got Mick's story in a few sentences. Mick said he had been paid one hundred dollars to scare the Newton brothers. Nothing more than that. He arrived on the ridge above their shack before dawn and waited until it got light enough to see the buildings, then he fired at their shack, keeping his shots high. All he wanted was to bring the men out of the house. He was to yell at them to get out of the county *pronto,* then he was to ride off.

They didn't show up, so, after he waited a while, he went down there and found the bodies in front of the door. They were dead then, so they'd been killed sometime during the night. He had no idea who had done it.

That's all he would say. He absolutely refused to identify the men who had hired him to scare the Newtons.

Both lawyers made their final statement to the jury. Neither said anything new. Pryor hammered mostly on the theme of reasonable doubt of Mick's guilt. If they had such a doubt, they must vote to acquit him.

The jurymen filed out of the room. They wouldn't

be out long, I thought. Mick would have been better off, if he had admitted it was Bromley who had hired him, and I was guessing that it was Bromley. The way I pictured it, he had gone to the Newton shack right after leaving the JM, killed the two men, and ridden away before Mick had reached the crest of the ridge.

Yes, I was guessing, but it made sense. One hundred dollars had gone to Mick, $900 had remained in Bromley's pocket. Maybe Mick had been hired just to scare the Newtons, not to kill them as Murdock had thought. Maybe he hadn't even known they were to be murdered, and he certainly had not known he was to be the scapegoat.

Hell, we'd never know for sure, I told myself for what must have been the hundreth time. Bromley couldn't talk and the chances were Mick and Gibson wouldn't. I was reasonably sure they were the only ones who knew the truth, and Mick didn't know all of it. I suspected that the association had left the arrangements in Gibson's and Bromley's hands. In any case, even if Mick really had intended to kill the Newtons, I felt he was telling the truth and that he had not done it.

I walked to a window. About half of the crowd had drifted into the hall. Perkins remained in a seat by the door. He'd be the first one out of the room when the verdict was announced, I thought.

I looked down at the homesteaders packed in front of the courthouse. Every homesteader in the county must have come to town for this. Perkins was right. I judged there were close to one hundred of them, most of them crowding around the big cottonwood near the street and others scattered between there and the front door of the courthouse.

Someone said: "Here they come." I turned to see the jurymen file back into the room. I took a long breath as I sat down beside Jim and Mick and John Pryor. We had waited a long time for the verdict. Now in a few seconds we'd know.

Chapter Thirty

"Not guilty."

The words were electrifying. For an instant we were shocked into a sort of immobility. I think we had all expected it, but the fact remained that there had been doubt. A relieved sigh swept the courtroom, then a burst of clapping. Most of the people here were townsmen and had known Mick from the time he'd been a child. Few if any really thought he was guilty.

Then everyone jumped up and started toward Mick to congratulate him. The exception was Perkins who bolted through the door and raced down the stairs to tell the homesteaders that the verdict was exactly what they had expected.

Jim and I were the first to shake Mick's hand because we were the closest to him, then Ellie was there. The crowd hung back for a moment while she hugged and kissed him. It was the first time in years I'd seen him kiss her. She said: "I'm so glad, Mick." He allowed himself the luxury of a grin as he said: "I'm kind of glad, too, Ma."

Jim and I shook hands with Pryor and told him he'd done a good job. He nodded gravely as if he knew he had, then he said to me: "Those bastards still outside waiting for him?"

"They were the last time I looked."

"My God, Bill, there's a thousand of them," he said. "You going to wait them out and keep him inside till they get tired and go home?"

"No," I answered. "Jim and I are taking him to Charley Three Horses's ranch."

"You can't do that," he said. "Not through that big crowd."

I wasn't sure we could, either, but I couldn't stay inside the courthouse with Mick. The homesteaders would come in after us if we did. There would be a lot of killing, and in the end they'd likely burn the courthouse and shoot us like dogs when we ran out.

On the other hand, they wouldn't expect us to walk outside with all of them standing there and get on our horses and ride out of town. I figured it was our best chance because we'd have a few seconds before they recovered from their surprise and realized that was exactly what we were doing. A few seconds might be enough if we moved fast.

"You watch us do it," I said. "Jim, go to the livery stable and saddle our horses. Bring all three of them to the front door of the courthouse."

Jim grinned. "On the double. John, personally I favor a good Methodist burial. See that I get it."

He plowed through the crowd to the door. Pryor shook his head. "I don't know about this, Bill. If I can help . . ."

"You've earned your pay," I said. "It's time Jim and I earned ours."

It was another fifteen or twenty minutes before the crowd in the courthouse melted away and I could get Mick downstairs to the jail. I returned his money and the knickknacks that had been in his pockets, then I gave him his Winchester and his .45.

"Don't fire a shot unless I start shooting," I said, "or you'll be right back in jail facing another murder charge. I'm guessing that we'll surprise those devils enough to get the bulge on them. We'll ride hell for leather right across the yard in front of the courthouse to the side street, and then swing into the end of Main Street and get on out of town. If anybody is in the way, we'll run them down."

"You don't have to take any chances and go with me," he said. "Just give me my horse."

"We'll go along just for the ride, Mick," I said.

All this time I'd been wondering where Murdock was. He wasn't anywhere in sight and I had kept hoping he'd show up. Now it was time to go and he still wasn't here. For the first time I began to feel jumpy. He had said he would help, and I had counted on him.

One man standing inside the courthouse firing three or four warning shots with a rifle would hold back the homesteaders for a few seconds and give us the margin we needed. At least it would help and could very possibly be the difference between getting out of town alive or all three of us winding up dead.

I turned to the gun rack and reached for the double-barrel shotgun. *It was gone.* I simply stood there with my right hand extended and stared at the rifles. I had only one shotgun that normally I would never dream of using. You just don't take a shotgun when you go after a wanted man, but it's the right kind of weapon for a mob.

It wasn't there and that's all there was to it. Mick asked: "What's the matter?"

"Nothing," I said. "Come on."

I grabbed a Winchester off the rack and wheeled outside into the hall. Murdock must have taken the shotgun, but why? And where was he? It had been there that morning. I knew it had been. *Damn him to hell*, I thought. That was like him, playing a lone hand just as he had when he'd sent some of his men after Bromley.

I hadn't been so mad since they laid the charge. I stomped down the hall, pausing at the window just long enough to see that Jim was out there with the horses and the crowd was scattered in front of the courthouse, some of them still around the big cottonwood next to Main Street and others a few feet on the other side of the horses.

"It'll take three or four long steps to reach your horse," I said. "Get on him and burn the breeze out of here. Jim and me will be right with you. Remember, no shooting unless I start it."

Mick nodded. We went through the front door together and we took the three long steps to our horses before they saw us and figured out what we were going to do. Several yelled: "There they are! Get the rope!" I was in my saddle on Diablo and Mick was swinging up when Murdock, who must have come around the corner of the building just as we cleared the door, let go with the shotgun.

Both barrels were loaded with buckshot and I have seen what buckshot does to a man, but still I wasn't quite prepared for it this time. Murdock literally blew off the top of Perkins's head. Another man a few feet from Perkins took the second load. The lower part of his face seemed to disintegrate.

I rode hard across the yard in front of the courthouse toward the side street, Mick and Jim a jump behind me. I heard the roar of angry shouts from the homesteaders, then some shooting, but none of the bullets seemed to be coming our way. I glanced back once. The crowd had started toward us like a great avalanche, but Murdock's shotgun blasts had taken out the leaders, the second man just as he grabbed for Mick's reins.

Another homesteader in front of me tried to stop me, but Diablo struck him and sent him spinning. Murdock had been hit, but he was still on his feet, a revolver in each hand. He was firing one, and then the other, and homesteaders were falling like grass in front of a mower. Even in the brief instant I glanced at Murdock, I saw him go down, the strength in those massive legs finally gone from him.

We were in the side street now. As we made the turn into Main Street, I realized that some bullets were ripping past our heads. At least I thought so. A little later I was sure because one of them sliced through the crown of my hat and another creased Mick's horse, making him buck for a moment before Mick got him lined out again.

We were moving fast now, straight out of Galt City toward the mountains. Murdock had taken the fight out of the mob. By the time we were on the edge of town, the firing stopped and nobody was chasing us.

I rode with them for a mile, then I signaled a stop.

I had to go back and see about Murdock. If anybody in the mob still wanted trouble, I'd see they got it. We pulled up, and I said: "Jim will go with you to Charley's ranch. What are you going to do?"

Mick wiped a sleeve across his face. "Dig up my wages and ride south, maybe to New Mexico. Tell Ma not to worry about me. I'll find work. Charley says I'm a good hand with horses."

"Write to her," I said. "We'll want to see you someday."

He nodded, kind of absent-mindedly, his gaze on the town we had just left. "I'll write," he said. He rubbed his chin, then he added, his voice filled with wonder: "I didn't know he knew about me."

"Sure he knew," I said. "He knew when you were a baby. Just the other night we were talking about you and he wished he could claim you, but it was too late."

Mick gave a short nod, his gaze still on the town. He frowned as if he had trouble comprehending this, then he said: "If he'd just said something so I'd have known that he . . ."

"He couldn't, Mick," I said. "He gave up any right to you a long time ago."

Then, surprisingly, Mick held out his hand. "Thanks," he said.

"Good luck," I said, and shook hands and wheeled my horse and rode back to Galt City.

I hadn't expected Mick to act that way. Now, as Murdock had said, it was too late to change things. Later, maybe, we would find Mick wherever he was working and our relationship might be different. Somehow, and I wasn't sure at all how and why, but somehow a great deal of the bitterness that had been stored up in Mick was gone.

When I got to town, I found that the homesteaders wanted no more trouble. They had forgotten all about burning the town. Three were dead, and two more badly wounded, and the rest just wanted to get out of Galt City and stay out, and that was exactly what I wanted. Murdock had been taken to Doc Ross's office. When I got there, Mrs. Ross met me at the door.

"We've sent for his wife," she said, "but he won't last long enough for her to get here. He's been asking for you. He's terribly wounded. The doctor can't get the bleeding stopped."

I went on into the office and through it to the back room that held a bed. Murdock was stretched out, his face more gray than ever. Now the expression on his gaunt face was that of death itself. I thought in my first glance he was gone; then I saw him stir.

"I'm here, Jake," I said. "Bill Lang."

He lifted a big hand. I took it as he said: "You got here just in time. It's getting dark." He swallowed as blood bubbled at the corners of his mouth. "The last bravado, Bill. Remember?"

It had been years since I had heard him say that. I remembered, all right, but somehow it didn't seem right. This wasn't an act of bravado. On the contrary, it had been an act of great courage, an act in which a man set out to give his life for others and he had known it when he had taken the shotgun from the gun rack and gone outside to wait.

"No, Jake . . ." I began, and stopped.

No use. Again I thought he was dead, then he asked: "Mick?"

"He's safe," I said. "Jim's going with him all the

way to the horse ranch. He said he wished he had known . . ."

Now I knew for sure there was no use. He was gone this time. I looked across the bed at Doc Ross. He nodded. "I don't know how he lived this long, Sheriff," the doctor said. "He was shot all to pieces."

"He kept their bullets from us," I said. "I guess they were all trying to cut him down."

Ross nodded. "They did it, too."

I went out and mounted Diablo and rode home. I didn't want to be there when Emily got there. Besides, I was kind of sick. So many things were popping back into my mind now that Murdock was dead, mostly how he had cut the Flynns to pieces that cold March day and saved my life.

Maybe I had ended up the solid one, but I don't think he died with the taste of ashes in his mouth. The fact was that I wouldn't be alive if it hadn't been for him. Twice it had happened, and this time I could not repay the debt. Maybe there wasn't any debt to repay; maybe he'd died the way he wanted to die.

When I put Diablo away in the barn and went into the house, Ellie was sitting by a window, staring into the street. She said without looking around: "Well?"

"Mick got away," I said. "He's all right. He promised to write to you. He shook hands with me and said thanks just as I left him."

She didn't say anything for a while. I sat down beside her and took her hands. "Jake's dead," I said. "They shot him to pieces. If he hadn't done what he did, I don't suppose we would have made it out of town."

"I know," she said. "I watched from a window in the courtroom. John Pryor was with me."

"The other night, when Jake and I were alone in my office," I said, "he told me there had never been a day after he married Emily when he hadn't wished he had you back."

Ellie looked at me then, her face grave. "He got exactly what he wanted and what he deserved, a white wife and a big ranch. He never would have been happy if he had kept me because he would always have wanted both of them." She shook her head at me reprovingly as if I should understand what I didn't seem to. "Bill, don't you see? I never would have been a . . . a woman if you hadn't come along. I was just a thing, a piece of furniture to Jake."

I had understood that before, but I had not realized how completely she understood it. I leaned forward and took her into my arms and kissed her long and hard. It's kind of strange, after all these years, I guess, but that's something I still like to do.

About the Author

Wayne D. Overholser won three Spur Awards from the Western Writers of America and has a long list of fine Western titles to his credit. He was born in Pomeroy, Washington, and attended the University of Montana, University of Oregon, and the University of Southern California before becoming a public schoolteacher and principal in various Oregon communities. He began writing for Western pulp magazines in 1936 and within a couple of years was a regular contributor to Street & Smith's *Western Story Magazine* and Fiction House's *Lariat Story Magazine*. *Buckaroo's Code* (1947) was his first Western novel and remains one of his best. In the 1950s and 1960s, having retired from academic work to concentrate on writing, he would publish as many as four books a year under his own name or a pseudonym, most prominently as Joseph Wayne. *The Violent Land* (1954), *The Lone Deputy* (1957), *The Bitter Night* (1961), and *Riders of the Sundowns* (1997) are among the finest of the Overholser titles. *The Sweet and Bit-*

ter Land (1950), *Bunch Grass* (1955), and *Land of Promises* (1962) are among the best Joseph Wayne titles, and *Law Man* (1953) is a most rewarding novel under the Lee Leighton pseudonym. Overholser's Western novels, whatever the byline, are based on a solid knowledge of the history and customs of the 19th Century West, particularly when set in his two favorite Western states, Oregon and Colorado. Many of his novels are first-person narratives, a technique that tends to bring an added dimension of vividness to the frontier experiences of his narrators and frequently, as in *Cast a Long Shadow* (1957), the female characters one encounters are among the most memorable. He wrote his numerous novels with a consistent skill and an uncommon sensitivity to the depths of human character. Almost invariably, his stories weave a spell of their own with their scenes and images of social and economic forces often in conflict and the diverse ways of life and personalities that made the American Western frontier so unique a time and place in human history.

BLOOD TRAIL TO KANSAS

ROBERT J. RANDISI

Ted Shea thinks he is a goner for sure. All the years
he's worked to build his Montana spread and fine
herd of prime beef means nothing if he can't sell
them. And with a vicious rustler and his gang of
cutthroats scaring all the hands, no one is willing to
take to the trail. Until Dan Parmalee drifts into town.
A gunman and gambler with a taste for long odds, he
isn't about to let a little hot lead part him from some
cold cash. But it doesn't take Dan long to realize this
isn't just any run. This is a...*Blood Trail to Kansas*.

ISBN 10: 0-8439-5799-9
ISBN 13: 978-0-8439-5799-0 $5.99 US/$7.99 CAN

NIGHT HAWK
STEPHEN OVERHOLSER

He came to the ranch with a mile-wide chip on his shoulder and no experience whatsoever. But it was either work on the Circle L or rot in jail, and he figured even the toughest labor was better than a life behind bars. He's got a lot to learn though, and he'd better learn it fast because he's about to face one of the toughest cattle drives in the country. They've got an ornery herd, not much water and danger everywhere they look. The greenhorn the cowboys call Night Hawk may not know much, but he does know this: The smallest mistake could cost him his life.

ISBN 10: 0-8439-5840-5
ISBN 13: 978-0-8439-5840-9 $5.99 US/$7.99 CAN

HEADING WEST
Western Stories
NOEL M. LOOMIS

Noel M. Loomis creates characters so real it's hard to believe they're fiction, and these nine stories vividly demonstrate his brilliant storytelling talent. Within this volume, you'll meet Big Blue Buckley, who proves it takes a "Tough *Hombre*" to build a railroad in the 1880s and "The St. Louis Salesman" who struggles with the harsh terrain of the Texas prairie. Most poignant of all is the dying Comanche warrior passing on the ways of his people in "Grandfather Out of the Past," a tale that won Loomis the prestigious Spur Award. Each story sweeps you back in time to the Old West as it really was.

ISBN 10: 0-8439-5897-9
ISBN 13: 978-0-8439-5897-3 $5.99 US/$7.99 CAN

To order a book or to request a catalog call:
1-800-481-9191
This book is also available at your local bookstore, or you can check out our Web site **www.dorchesterpub.com** where you can look up your favorite authors, read excerpts, or glance at our discussion forum to see what people have to say about your favorite books.